DÆMOS RISING

THE CHANGING FACE OF KATE LETHBRIDGE-STEWART

The cover illustration portrays the first KATE
LETHBRIDGE-STEWART, before she became Head of
Scientific Research at the Unified Intelligence Taskforce
(UNIT).

Also available in the Telos Adventure series:

OLIVE HAWTHORNE AND THE DÆMONS OF DEVIL'S END

SIL AND THE DEVIL SEEDS OF ARODOR

This book is sold subject to the condition that it shall not, by way of trade, be lent, re-sold, hired out or otherwise circulated without the publisher's consent in any form of binding or cover other than that in which it is published.

A TELOS ADVENTURE

DÆMOS RISING

Based on the Reeltime Pictures drama *Dæmos Rising* by David J Howe by arrangement with Reeltime Pictures Limited

DAVID J HOWE

Telos Editor : Sam Stone

Telos Publishing is a division of Telos Publishing Ltd,
www.telos.co.uk

First published in Great Britain by
Telos Publishing Ltd, 2019

ISBN 978 1 84583 977 2

Dæmos Rising © 2004, 2019 David J Howe

Cover Art © 2019, Andrew-Mark Thompson
Cover Photographs © 2004, Robin Prichard, David J Howe

All original characters from 'The Dæmons' © 1971, Robert Sloman and Barry Letts.
Captain Cavendish © 1994 Marc Platt
Kate Lethbridge-Stewart © 1994 Marc Platt
'Time Hunter' format © 2004 David J Howe and Stephen James Walker

The moral right of the author has been asserted.

Dæmos Rising is based on, and expands upon, the 2004 Reeltime Pictures drama production *Dæmos Rising* released on DVD by Koch Media and available from www.timetraveltv.com. It also spins off from the 1971 BBC *Doctor Who* adventure 'The Dæmons'. All characters are used with permission of the relevant rights owners. This book has not been licensed or approved by the BBC or any of its affiliates.

British Library Cataloguing in Publication Data. A catalogue record for this book is available from the British Library.

While we have tried to emulate the look of the '70s Target Books, there are some details which eluded us . . . we hope this doesn't detract from your pleasure in this edition.

Dedicated to the Voice of the Dæmons, the magnificent Stephen Thorne, who died at the end of May 2019. His voice was echoing through my head as I wrote this book! RIP.

Printed and bound in Great Britain by 4Edge Ltd

CONTENTS

	Foreword	7
	Prologue	11
PART ONE		
1	The End of Time	21
2	The Book	25
3	Memories of Times Past	32
4	Reading the Book	35
5	London 2586	39
6	Tea with Olive	41
7	The Attack	47
PART TWO		
1	The Cottage	55
2	Cavendish	63
3	The Statue	68
4	Lost in Time	69
5	Tea with Douglas	72
6	Night Terrors	79
7	The Collection	87
8	Meet the Ghost	93
9	Doubles	97
10	Charm Offensive	100
PART THREE		
1	The Caverns	109
2	The Dæmon	116
3	Discussions with the Devil	121
4	Endgame	126
	Epilogue	129
	About the Author	131

Aeons ago, a mighty race toyed with life as children might play with ants. Earth was one such playground, but an emissary to that world became trapped. Blind and ignorant people with a lust for power released the sleeping devil and demanded of him a final judgement. But Azal was destroyed, his energies turned inward ... dissipating deep into the Earth and in time luring the ambitious, the greedy and the broken. In the void between time the devils waited ... patiently ... to be summoned again ... to pass judgement on the Earth ...

Foreword

The book you hold in your hands is a slightly different take on the story which made it to DVD as *Dæmos Rising* back in 2004. For a start, one hopes that when you read the tale within, you will not literally become sucked into the future or the past, or summon Dæmons from a distant world to pass judgement on you...

The background to *Dæmos Rising* is interesting though, so please indulge me as I explain, as best I can, what happened.

Back in 2004, and following the success of the range of *Doctor Who* novellas, Telos Publishing decided to create a spin-off series featuring two of the characters created by Daniel O'Mahony for his *Doctor Who* novella, *The Cabinet of Light*. These were Honoré Lechasseur, a Time Sensitive, and Emily Blandish, a Time Channeller. Together they could travel through time, following people's 'time snakes' and emerge at any point in their past or future. Thus by 'hopping' from person to person they could travel pretty much anywhere in time.

When Stephen James Walker and I devised the 'Time Hunter' series and concepts, we always knew that we wanted a circular plot arc, and that the 'untold' truth about what was going on would be revealed at the end of the series of books. Thus, in 2004, we had a pretty good idea about what was driving the series and where it would end up. One benefit to this of course, was that all the books we commissioned were true to this background, whether the authors knew what the background was or not—as editors, we made sure of it.

Enter Producer Keith Barnfather, who in 2004 approached me to write a script for his Reeltime Pictures company to produce. A *Doctor Who* spin off adventure, which originally was planned to feature the Sea Devils, and which would be set in a cottage and caves (as these were locations which Keith knew were available to use). Using the Sea Devils fell through because, also in 2004, unknown to us, the BBC were starting to gear up for production of a new television series of *Doctor Who*, and as part of that were contacting the various rights holders to see what past *Doctor Who* creations might be available to use. These included the Sea Devils and Silurians, owned by the estate of Malcolm Hulke. The estate, understandably, were excited by the BBC's approach, and so when Keith also approached them for rights, were reluctant to say yes, unless the BBC also said yes: but of course the BBC owned no rights in any part of the production which Keith was planning, and had no reason to say 'yes' at all, and so we had to think again.

For Telos' 'Time Hunter' series, we had secured the use of the characters of the Dæmons from Barry Letts and Robert Sloman (and later in the series we also gained permission from Chris Boucher to use the Fendahl) so I knew that potentially Keith could gain the same agreement from them. Thus we changed the basis of the script Keith wanted from Sea Devils to Dæmons, but still retained the cottage and cave locations.

Because at the time I was heavily into the planning of the 'Time Hunter' series, I wanted to try and bring that into the mix of the film as well, so with Keith's blessing I created another time sensitive (our elusive unnamed Ghost), and crafted the script around the Dæmon Mastho's first appearance on Earth. This was following the Dæmon Azal's appearance in the *Doctor Who* adventure 'The Dæmons' where he self-destructed rather than handing over his powers, or destroying the Dæmons' experiment: Humanity.

As it happened, the final book in the 'Time Hunter' series, *Child of Time*, written by myself and George Mann, tells the story of Mastho's second and third—

8

and final—appearances on Earth, and what happens . . . It also wraps up the story of Honoré and Emily, hopefully in a way which was clever yet satisfying to those who had stuck with the series of novellas. I'm still very proud of what we did there, and hope that *Doctor Who* fans will seek out and enjoy the adventures in the spirit in which they were intended: an adjunct to *Doctor Who* itself.

So coming to this novelisation of *Dæmos Rising*, I had the opportunity to neaten things up, and to bring this massive plot arc to some sort of resolution.

I see the events as taking place in three distinct segments.

·   ·   ·   ·   ·

'Part One' is the television *Doctor Who* story, 'The Dæmons', in which we learn of Azal, and of the Dæmons great experiment on Earth: the creation and development of Humanity; an experiment which is allowed to continue as Azal is, at the end, destroyed by the 'alien' human emotion of love, when Jo Grant offers herself as victim instead of the Doctor.

·   ·   ·   ·   ·

'Part Two' is *Dæmos Rising*, where we see the summoning of a second Dæmon, Mastho, to cast judgement on the Earth. But on this occasion, the events are being manipulated behind the scenes by a cabal called the Sodality . . . you will find out more about them in this book!

·   ·   ·   ·   ·

'Part Three' is *Child of Time*, wherein we discover the Dæmons' true reasons for creating their experiment in the first place, and how the Sodality have managed to corrupt it, and indeed, how they played into the Dæmons' hands all along.

·   ·   ·   ·   ·

If you enjoy this book, and want to find out how the story ends, then seek out *Child of Time*, available as an ebook edition from Telos Publishing.

There is also a short story I penned for the Reeltime Pictures drama *White Witch of Devil's End* called 'Dæmos Returns' which tells of a further encounter that Olive Hawthorne (a character from 'The Dæmons' on television) has with the residual power of the Dæmons. This again uses as a background the overall story arc which is being used again here. The story is expanded and developed in Telos Publishing's novelisation of *White Witch of Devil's End* (called *The Dæmons of Devil's End*).

In the meantime, settle back, and enjoy the ride as we find out how events progressed following 'The Dæmons', and how a certain book of Dæmonic psyonic incantations fell into the wrong hands, and triggered the events of *Dæmos Rising* . . .

Oh, and incidentally, we had no idea when we made *Dæmos Rising* that the book of psyonic science, created by artist Bob Covington for the production, would go on to appear in another Reeltime Pictures drama, *White Witch of Devil's End*, some fourteen years later!

David J Howe,
March 2019

Prologue

The church had been blown up.

At least that's what Corporal Fitch thought had happened. Working for UNIT, you saw all manner of strange things. Blown up things. Blown out things. Things which looked like they had been blown in.

It was best not to ask. Just get in, do the job, and get back out again.

Some of Fitch's colleagues had spoken of missions they had been on. Things they had seen. Much of which Fitch thought were embellished to the point of being science fiction, but which always had a strange ring of truth about them.

And then there was the Archive.

Best not to talk about the Archive.

That was real Black Ops territory. Need to know. Top security clearance.

So Fitch often didn't know what to believe. He had seen some things himself. He had been stationed with a troop out near Nuton when something fell to Earth there. The power station was put on alert, lots of senior bods turned up, and he ended up guarding what looked like a gigantic squashed gourd poking up out of the shingle on the local beach. No idea why. Need to know.

That was always the response.

'Need to know.'

Why were a load of shop mannequins brought in for investigation?

'Need to know.'

Why did they go out and blow up a load of perfectly good caves in Derbyshire?

'Need to know.'

Why were bazookas and other heavy artillery called

to defend or attack a church in Wiltshire?

'Need to know.'

To be honest, Fitch was getting somewhat fed up of 'Need to know'. He really would rather know . . .

And now he was sorting through rubble and fallen beams in said church, now part-demolished by goodness knows what.

He pulled his beige beret off his head and mopped his brow. It was hot work.

He idly kicked at a piece of fallen stone and it clattered away into the gloom in the corners of what used to be the church's catacombs, now a hazardous mess of brick and mortar. A voice hailed him from the doorway.

'Hello? Is there anyone there?'

Fitch stepped gingerly across the floor and saw a woman peering in at him. She could have been in her thirties or late twenties . . . pinched face and with a cloak pinned to her shoulders.

'Ah, hello, there you are,' she said with a smile. As she smiled, her eyes crinkled and Fitch knew instinctively that he could trust her.

There was a movement at her feet and a black cat curled past her and stood for a moment surveying the damage, before heading out again.

'Oh, don't mind him,' said the woman. 'Rhad will be back. There's no doubt mice and rats to be hunting.'

Fitch reached the doorway. 'It's not safe here, miss,' he said.

'Hawthorne,' said the woman. 'Olive Hawthorne. I live here.'

Fitch reached for her outstretched hand and gave it a cursory shake.

'Here?' he said, looking around the broken church. 'Not sure it's safe to live here.'

'Oh I don't mean "here" literally,' Olive said. 'The village. I live in the village.'

'Ah,' Fitch nodded and stepped out into the sunlight

beside Olive.

'Nasty business,' the woman continued. 'Glad it's all over.'

Fitch nodded, and pulled the door as shut as he could behind him. 'That should hold it until the boys can get a cordon up.'

Fitch looked at Miss Hawthorne who was standing beside him looking very expectant.

'Can I . . . help with something Miss?' he asked.

Olive grinned. 'Tea.'

'Tea?'

'Yes. I was going to ask if you wanted some tea.'

Fitch looked around. 'Well . . . I'm on duty, Miss.'

'Oh, don't be silly. No-one is going to begrudge you a drink. And besides . . . there's no-one else here!'

Fitch had to agree that she was right. He had come in early as there was no-one else around. He did have his instructions though. To carry out an initial inspection and to mark and cordon anything which seemed of interest.

When he asked what 'of interest' meant, his Sergeant, Yates, smiled, and said 'You'll know it when you see it.'

'Tea would be lovely, Miss,' he said, smiling at Olive.

They walked together around the ruins of the church. The cat wandered through the bushes, and pounced on imaginary mice, moving leaves and grass.

'My cottage is just down there,' said Olive. 'I'll pop down and get you a cup now.'

'That's very kind, miss,' said Fitch.

They had reached another doorway into the church. From the information Fitch had, this led to the private quarters of the Vicar there, a certain Mr Magister.

He nodded to the door. 'Got to check in here now,' he said. 'Won't take long.'

Olive smiled and headed off down the path towards her cottage.

What a nice woman, thought Fitch. Shame that most people seemed to be hostile and unhelpful.

He mentally shrugged to himself and tried the handle to the door.

Locked.

He reached into his pocket and pulled out his trusty UNIT issue skeleton keys. There wasn't a lock made which these wouldn't open.

After a minute or so of trying the various picks and jiggling the lock, it clicked, and the door swung open.

Fitch stepped out of the sunshine and into the chilly gloom of the apartment beyond.

· · · · ·

'You'll know it when you see it.'

Yates' words echoed in Fitch's mind when he saw the large, leather-bound book sitting on a lectern to one side of the room.

To be honest, to Fitch's trained eye, it looked like the place had not been lived in for some time. Especially not by anyone called Magister.

The table had a pile of unopened post for a Canon Smallwood. There were a few, but not many, religious books on the shelves. A selection of robes for various masses through the year. All dusty and unworn.

There was absolutely nothing to suggest that anyone called Magister had ever been there.

In one corner there was a strange *empty* area, as though something about the size of a large cabinet had stood there for a time, but which was now missing. There were marks in the dust on the floor, but no scuff marks, so it hadn't been dragged somewhere else.

Fitch wondered how something of that size could possibly have been moved. Indeed, how it could have been removed from the room: the door was quite small, and the windows were also tiny, with old fashioned stained glass and leading intact.

But the book on the lectern.

Fitch reached out a hand to touch it, and in the cool

atmosphere it felt warm. Was it leather? Or some other substance? It was hard to tell.

Fitch lifted the heavy cover, and noted that the pages seemed to be covered with an ancient script, interspersed with drawings and paintings.

The text seemed to blur before his eyes. Not only could he not read it, but he couldn't even see it to be able to read it.

He turned a few more pages, and the strange blurred sensation in his eyes moved to his brain. He felt a little fuzzy, as though he had been drinking.

He squinted at the page. Maybe . . .

A little voice wormed into his head. A nagging thought that if he really focussed, then he would be able to read. And all he had to do was to read a small portion, and then everything would be so much better.

Fitch looked around the room. Everything was quiet and still, but he had a sense that something was poised, watching him. Waiting.

He turned another page, and a sense of happiness engulfed him. He was doing the right thing.

He looked at one of the images.

A massive, muscular beast-like humanoid, covered with coarse hair, and with two curling horns emerging from its head, was holding the figure of a man between its hands. But the man's body was split in two, as though the beast had torn him apart.

Fitch frowned. He wasn't meant to worry about that. Something was urging him on, to read something somewhere else in the book.

He turned another page.

The door behind him suddenly opened and a bright voice said, 'Ah, there you are.'

The strange foggy feeling abruptly lifted from Fitch. The urge to read vanished, leaving a strange, nagging, *empty* feeling.

He shut the book, and turned to see Miss Hawthorne proffering a steaming hot cup of tea to him.

'Thank . . . thank you Miss,' he said, fully shaken from whatever had fallen on him.

He took the cup and saucer and sipped at the hot tea. It slid down his throat, which he realised had gone dry, as had his lips.

Miss Hawthorne was looking at the book.

'*That* was Magister's,' she said with a note of warning in her voice. 'I wondered where it had gone.'

Fitch nodded and took another sip of tea.

'That's why I'm here, miss,' he said. 'To make sure that things are properly secured.'

Miss Hawthorne looked at him carefully.

'There were things abroad in this village, dark forces, the likes of which are best kept unknown.'

Fitch nodded again.

'Well, they will be kept unknown,' he said. 'UNIT's orders.'

With a backwards glance at the book, he ushered Miss Hawthorne out of the room and back into the sunshine. He blew on the tea and finished the cup.

'Thank you miss,' he said, handing it back to Olive.

He pulled the door closed, and locked it again.

'We'll keep it safe,' he said with a wink.

With a cheery wave, Fitch set off back to his jeep. There he had some secure tape, and plastic bags into which the book would fit.

Their scientific adviser had also provided some sort of electronic doohicky of a box into which anything really 'special' could be placed. And the book would be the first thing in there.

·   ·   ·   ·   ·

Olive stood and watched the soldier go.

She frowned gently.

There was still danger in this place. The runes showed it. And that book was part of it all. It would be good to see it gone.

Another magickal item of power taken out of the reach of those who might abuse it.

Olive sighed and looked at the teacup in her hands.

The tealeaves in the base of the cup had formed into a shape. A circle with two protuberances emerging from the top, a little like horns.

Olive frowned again. There was more trouble coming. She could feel it.

But this time she would be ready.

PART ONE

1
The End of Time

A breeze stirred the grey dust into eddies across the empty plaza. The skies were full of grey clouds, and an occasional drizzle fell, dampening the ground and turning it a darker grey.

2050 was not a good year for humanity. The start of the rise of the Sodality.

Suddenly, across the open space between shattered buildings which reached for the skies like broken teeth, the shape of a man appeared between the broken rubble.

He raced across the plaza and scurried behind a wall where a young girl was waiting for him.

The two humans crouched still, trying to control their breath, and to be as silent as they could.

From the other side of the open space, a darker shadow detached itself from the wall.

There was an echoing sound, faint, but like concrete rubbing against concrete. A slow scraping noise.

The man put his finger up against his lips.

The girl nodded.

He slowly poked his head around the wall so he could see the other side of the plaza.

There it was.

As he watched, the shape moved, slowly, towards the centre of the plaza. It was like some sort of animal, but none created by nature. Its skin was like stone, riven with cracks, and its massive horned head was worn and rubbed as though by centuries of wind and rain.

It paused in the plaza, its head moving back and forth as though trying to scent the humans it had been chasing.

The man ducked his head back.

The two humans heard a clatter of stone hooves

against broken cobblestones, and then the whooshing of stone wings against the air. Then there was silence.

The man popped his head back around the wall again. Nothing.

He realised that he had been holding his breath, and let it out with a whoosh.

'It's gone,' he said. 'For the moment.'

The girl studied the man closely. 'You know they're tracking us, Andy?'

He looked at her. Her long light brown hair was matted, but her skin was clean. Blue eyes looked at him from a petite pretty face.

'I know,' he said. 'But we're one step ahead.'

'The High Executioner is determined to wipe us all out,' the girl said. 'She's insane.'

'She has her own agenda, Laura,' said Andy.

'So, what now?' said Laura, standing and brushing her trousers as though this action could remove the stains and grey dust which permeated everything in this time zone.

Andy didn't remark how pointless this gesture was. He looked around. 'We have knowledge, and that's dangerous to the Sodality. I also think we might be the last.'

He looked down at Laura, his dark eyes piercing her. She often thought he looked a little like a film star, with a balding head, and neatly trimmed beard.

'So we need to run again?' Laura looked at him seriously.

Andy looked around again. 'We can, but to do that we need to find someone to facilitate . . .'

His eyes caught a movement the other side of the Plaza. 'Shh . . .' he warned, and ducked down again.

With a clatter, perhaps the same, perhaps a different gargoyle creature landed on the cobbles. It raised its great head and swung back and forth.

Then it headed straight for Andy and Laura.

They crouched behind the wall, listening as the hooves struck the stone of the ground, coming closer and closer.

Then, with a rush of air, the creature headbutted the

wall, causing it to crack and bow in the middle. Bricks fell from the top, just missing Laura.

She let out a squeal.

'Run!' shouted Andy, and grabbing Laura's hand they set off through an arched passageway.

The stone creature gave chase, slipping and raising sparks from its hooves as it raced after them.

At one corner it crashed into the wall, bringing a torrent of grey dust and brick down on top of it. But this barely slowed it down. It shook off the dust like a huge dog shaking off water. There was barely a beat before the creature gave chase again.

Andy and Laura kept changing direction, taking random passages and streets, trying to keep some distance between themselves and the gargoyle, but it was exhausting.

They burst out into a small area beside a large river. This had once been called the Thames and had been a beautiful stretch of clean water running through the city. But now it was dirty and grey, like the rest of the world, and full of broken masonry and rubbish. There was no life left in what had formerly been known as London.

Andy spotted that the one remaining bridge over the river was nearby, and in the few moments available, focussed his energy on searching for a time snake.

There!

On the other side of the river was the distinct shape and form of a person's time snake. It unravelled from humans like some sort of visible projection of their lives: forward and backwards in time. Only a Time Sensitive could see them, and Andy was one of that dwindling group of individuals, granted this power by whatever meddling the Sodality had undertaken through history.

The time snake laid out a person's lifeline: a glowing stream of light-like particles which connected an individual to their past, their present and their future . . . assuming they had any.

'Come on,' Andy said. 'Over the bridge.'

As the stone creature careered into view behind them, Laura and Andy raced along the embankment and up a set of crumbling stairs towards the bridge.

On the other side of the river they could see the shape of St Paul's Cathedral silhouetted against the shattered sky. It was grey and broken, but still triumphant, and the massive dome was intact.

Keeping his eye on the time snake, Andy hurried across the bridge, avoiding the edges where the ancient balustrades had fallen into the river below, and trying to dodge the holes which dotted the surface.

Behind them the gargoyle kept coming. It was relentless in its pursuit, and unlike the human couple, tireless.

They reached the other side of the Thames, and Andy hurried down another set of steps, and into another warren of passages along the side of the river.

It was here he had seen the snake.

It called to him somehow. He knew that this was their only way out as once one of those stone gargoyle things got your scent, there was only one way to escape: through time.

The passages opened up again into a small square, where a man dressed in a plain outfit was hurriedly trying to open a door.

Exhausted and breathless, Andy looked at the man carefully. He was scared, but his time snake extended forward as well as backwards. He would not die this day.

'This is it,' said Andy, grasping Laura's hand. 'Now!'

As the stone gargoyle came rushing around the corner, the man managed to open the door and hurried inside, slamming it behind him.

Outside, the creature came to a skidding halt. It seemed to sniff the air, but there was no scent left.

On the wall beside the doorway, a crackling, electric blue light crawled, marking the shape of what could have been a man and a woman.

But they were gone.

2
The Book

'Sir!'

The young recruit on duty gave Captain Cavendish a smart salute.

Cavendish returned it with a nod, and continued past the checkpoint and into the building.

Cavendish walked past the normal civilian entry doors and stopped at an inconsequential metal door set into the wall of the building.

It was deliberately designed to look like absolutely nothing of importance. Just a service area, or maybe the boiler room.

He pulled out his pass and waved it in front of one of the bricks beside the door. The hidden sensor detected it, and the door clicked once.

Cavendish then waved the pass on a different brick, and the door clicked a second time.

This procedure was drilled into anyone who needed access. The first sensor activated an electric current which flowed through the door and the handle. Anyone trying to open the door after just swiping once would receive a very nasty electric shock. Not enough to kill but certainly sufficient to disable someone for a limited time. Time enough for the alarm to be raised and for UNIT soldiers to pour into the area to arrest the trespasser.

The second sensor deactivated the current and opened the door fully. Only a few trusted officers knew this and had access to the area. Cavendish was one of them.

Cavendish grasped the handle and pulled the door open. It opened outwards as it could then not be easily battered in from outside. Another precaution that showed they were taking no chances—and for good reason.

Inside was a short corridor which led to another room. This was lined with mops and buckets, and a wooden shelf unit stood on one side with a couple of tins of paint standing on it. For all the world it was a small cleaner's closet.

That was what it was meant to look like.

Cavendish reached out to one of the mops, and moved the handle sharply to the left. There was a click, and the room juddered slightly as it began to descend. The only evidence that it was moving was a faint bar of light which repeatedly rose up the small window set into the door of the room.

After a minute or so, the room juddered again, and Cavendish opened the door which previously had led to the short brick corridor and outside.

Now it opened onto a polished steel corridor, with a door at the end, beside which another soldier was seated.

When he saw Cavendish, the soldier stood and saluted sharply.

'Sir!'

Cavendish saluted back and approached.

'Pass, sir?'

Cavendish handed over his pass, and the soldier looked at it carefully. Checking the dates, the signature, and finally the photograph of Captain Cavendish which adorned it.

When he was satisfied, he handed the pass back to the Captain, and opened the door.

Cavendish nodded and strode into the area beyond.

Here there was another guard, and another table. He too checked Cavendish's pass, and eventually handed it back.

Then finally, Cavendish was allowed to enter the facility.

Cavendish thought all this was crazy. So much

security on the way in, but next to none on the way out. And just one man at each station. It was as though they had never encountered someone like the Master before. Number one on their wanted list, the Master could so easily have got inside and out again with very little effort. Even though he was so sought after, that the whole organisation was on alert for him.

Why was he called the Master? Cavendish had his own ideas about that. He was a master of disguise, and could be standing right next to you before you knew it. He was also a master hypnotist, and again, before you knew it, you would be helping him with whatever scheme or scam he was running at that moment.

But these things were all the concern of the top brass. A lowly Captain like Cavendish was not privy to the discussions that presumably took place.

Cavendish instead felt neglected and forgotten. A Captain in UNIT who was on his way up and up . . . successful missions, great rescues . . . but then . . . following what was being described as 'The University Incident', he was suddenly passed over for promotion and assigned a series of dreary office jobs.

'The University Incident' . . . well that was an interesting way to describe it.

Cavendish paused at the main desk of the facility. All was quiet as customary, and the man at the desk was, as usual, reading a book.

'Ok George,' said Cavendish.

The man, George, flicked his eyes up from the page and nodded. Then he returned to his book.

Cavendish moved on.

This was UNIT's Black Archive. A storehouse of all the items it found, confiscated and didn't destroy in the line of action. But there were some partially destroyed items here as well.

Anything which seemed *alien* ended up here. Anything strange or beyond human understanding.

Sometimes the boffins tried to disassemble the items,

trying to find out what they were or how they worked, but often their *modus operandi* was completely beyond comprehension.

Cavendish moved down one of the aisles. Either side of him were metal shelves and cages. Each containing the objects.

He passed a box in which nestled a spherical globe made from some sort of green-tinged plastic. A meteorite apparently, but like no other that had been seen.

Another cage held a selection of plastic store manikins. Legs and arms and bodies all disassembled. But next to this, were three arms taken from the dummies. They looked normal enough, but the hands had a strange seam running around the knuckle area, and one was open; hinged down to reveal the nozzle of what could be a blaster hidden within the hand.

Robots. That's what everyone thought. But on further investigation, they turned out to be completely solid plastic dummies. No articulation or inner workings at all.

Everything in here was like that. Unexplainable.

Further down the passage there was another cage, and inside were five or six silver spherical objects arranged in a pyramid shape.

Cavendish looked at these and shuddered.

He remembered them well.

· · · · ·

There was a roar and the yeti launched itself across the University Square.

Cavendish, standing alongside the entranced 'Chillys'—Students who had become enraptured and controlled by whatever the thing was that had first invaded New World University's computer systems, and from there the rest of the staff and students—looked on as the Brigadier, accompanied by his daughter, walked into view.

The silver spheres were on a dais beside him, and his mind was full of confusion and noise and the voice of a power called the Great Intelligence.

There were distant shots. Gunfire.

The Vice Chancellor of the University, a lady called Victoria Waterfield, was there. And a journalist well known to UNIT called Sarah Jane Smith was hanging around too.

And the yeti!

A mythical creature from the Himalayas, careering across a modern-day University campus. And controlled, somehow, by the silver balls . . .

But worse than that, the yeti's hands seemed to be guns. They emitted a stream of smoke-like substance which coalesced into web.

Yeti monsters spinning killing webs . . . you couldn't make it up.

Cavendish stood there. His mind reeling.

He was told to pick up a sphere and 'present' it to the Brigadier. He didn't want to . . . but . . .

The bleeping of the silver spheres echoed in his head.

•   •   •   •   •

Cavendish rested his hand against the metal cage. He felt dizzy. This happened from time to time, but it was normal. His doctor had assured him of that.

He sucked in a deep breath and composed himself. Now. What was he here to do?

He continued down the cage-lined passageway, and turned into another. At the far end, a further passageway extended, but here the cages were mostly empty. This was where the new acquisitions came.

In one of the cages was a book.

Cavendish quickly checked the passages, but as usual they were deserted. This had become something of a ritual for him. A way of coping with all that UNIT had thrown at him.

If he could actually touch . . . actually keep some of these objects and artefacts, then the nightmares seemed somehow more real to him, and in making them real, he was able to understand them and push them away.

There was nothing worse than waking with a nameless dread that something unknown was coming for you. That there were things beyond human understanding.

To actually have some of these objects in his possession helped. He then *knew* they were real, and thus the nameless dread of the unknown was lessened.

As a soldier, Cavendish had lived his life on the solid certainty of a gun and law and order. Seeing things which made no sense unsettled him. Made him worse.

So he justified his actions with the salve of his own sanity.

He quickly opened the cage with the small skeleton key that he had had made for the purpose, and gently laid his hand on the book.

When the book had first come in, some twenty years ago, Cavendish had still been in nappies. But on joining UNIT, he had become fascinated by its story.

It had been located by Captain Fitch (now retired) at one of the operations centres during the investigations of the Master. Seems that the Master had blown up a church, with reports of moving statues and devils roaming the surrounding woods. Indeed, a prominent historian had been killed there too . . . no doubt all part of whatever plan the Master was hatching.

But he had been captured and taken away to some secure offshore facility, and what remained of the church sealed up and thoroughly explored and 'decontaminated' by UNIT.

This was where the book had been found. It had arrived sealed in one of the special containers as it was supposedly dangerous. But then all of the things here were supposed to be dangerous. Quite how a jar of jelly babies could be seen as that, or the head of a gargoyle, or even a plastic dummy . . . but the belief was there and so they were locked up safely. That was, until Cavendish had taken selected items into his own custody.

As Cavendish stood there with his hand on the book, it was as though he could hear voices in his head. Soft and alluring. Telling him that everything would be all right, and that he was right to take the book. There was no problem.

He smiled to himself. This was what it was all about. Making him feel better.

He reached in and picked up the book. It was big, perhaps eighteen inches by ten inches and about five inches thick.

As his hands closed around it, so the feeling of warmth increased.

Cavendish smiled and hurriedly placed the book under his jacket. Buttoning it up, and cinching the belt tightly.

There would be no checks. There never were.

He closed and relocked the cage, then headed back down the passages towards the exit desk.

This time there was no-one there. The book was lying on the table, propped open at whatever page the guard had reached.

Cavendish headed for the door, and was through it and heading back towards the lift while the guard there threw a half-hearted salute at his back.

Through the next door, into the lift room, ignoring the second guard.

Cavendish operated the lift again and it rose up.

Moments later Cavendish was emerging into the dusty sunlight.

He strode back to his car, the book warm and comforting against his body.

He knew he had done the right thing.

He knew it. The book was meant to be his, just like all the other objects were.

3
Memories of Times Past

A breeze blew fresh, clean air across green fields. It was sunny and bright, and the sounds of children playing echoed across the grass.

A small child ran along a path, without a care in the world, and leaped over a stile into a small wooded area.

There was an electric hum and buzz, as though a generator had been started, and a vivid blue light flickered unnoticed in the trail of the child.

From nowhere, Andy and Laura stepped into the time zone. Their bodies were covered in crawling blue electricity which snapped and sparked and died away, evaporating in the warm air.

Laura looked around. 'Well this is different!'

Andy had his head down and his hands were on his knees. He was breathing heavily.

'Why does it always do that to me!' he said.

He took in some deep breaths to try and shake the sick feeling.

Whenever he and Laura jumped through time, it hit him like the worst travel sickness ever. Laura was never affected, but then she was a Time Channeller and was able to focus in on the time snake, locating the specific place and time that she wanted to emerge. If she was alone, then this talent was dormant. It took the physical presence of a Time Sensitive to locate the time snake in the first place, and to enable them both to travel. They couldn't do this without each other and they were both aware of it.

Laura looked up at the blue sky, stepping away from Andy. She spun in a small circle.

'This is more like it. No greyness. No destruction.'

'Where are we? Or rather when?'

'It's earlier,' said Laura. 'There's some kids playing nearby, probably one of those was our man.'

'So what, maybe sixty years earlier?'

Laura nodded. 'Something like that anyway. What a difference.'

Andy looked around. He was starting to feel better. At least they were out of immediate danger.

'We need to find some more people,' said Andy. 'That's if we want to stand any chance of getting somewhere more useful.'

Laura nodded. 'I think the town is that way,' she said, pointing to where some smoke spiralled into the sky.

Andy and Laura headed off away from the copse of woodland and towards the smoke.

Before long they arrived at the first houses. Standard English brick built houses from the twentieth century. Andy did some calculations in his head. They had been in the year 2050, which was when the Sodality had poisoned the air and were hunting for Time Channellers and Sensitives. The man they had travelled back with had been in his seventies, so they were perhaps now sixty years earlier. So, 1990s?

It looked about right. Andy noticed a rubbish bin at the side of the road and went over to it. After a moment he returned to Laura brandishing a grubby newspaper.

'It's 2003.'

'Well that's not too bad, is it?'

Andy shook his head. 'No.'

'When did we want to get to?' asked Laura.

Andy sighed. 'You know, I have no idea.'

'Not helpful.'

'Sorry. It's hard enough trying to fight these people in one timezone, but now that they are spreading out, trying to wipe us out everywhere . . .'

Laura touched his arm. 'Don't worry. At least we're away from that thing here.'

'I know. But for how long?'

The two friends continued walking along the street. Before long, it opened into a village green, with a large church sitting at the far side. Off on one side of the green was a public house. 'The Cloven Hoof' read the sign above the door.

Andy pushed the door but it was closed.

'Wrong time of day for that,' said a voice.

Andy and Laura turned and saw that they were being addressed by a smart woman in a pair of *pince nez* glasses. She was wearing a cloak, and pushing a bicycle. Andy thought that maybe she was in her fifties or sixties.

'I'm sorry,' said Andy. 'We seem to have come out without...'

The woman smiled. Andy could sense that she was kind, and he focussed a little harder to see if he could sense her time snake. But there was some sort of a block.

She smiled again. 'It's half past nine in the morning. And you'll have to try harder than that to make sense of me, young man.'

Andy frowned, suddenly feeling uneasy.

'It's all right,' said the woman. 'I can tell you're not from these parts.'

She turned and started to push her bicycle up the street. After a moment she stopped and turned to them.

'Well come on then, if you want a cup of tea. And some explanations. I can tell that you want explanations.'

'That's very kind of you,' said Laura. 'Thank you Mrs...'

'It's Miss... Miss Hawthorne. But you can call me Olive, dear.'

4
Reading the Book

Cavendish slammed the door to his car.

He was still furious from the morning's meeting. How could they do that to him? To him?

He strode down the driveway to the cottage, pausing to admire the gardens and their vibrant colours.

He sighed. At least he had this. His own retreat in the country. Somewhere that no-one, not even his UNIT overlords knew about.

He entered the cottage and headed to the kitchen to make himself a cup of tea. As the water heated, he watched as the steam rose from the spout, creating rivulets of water on the glass cabinets.

His mind wandered back to that morning. To the summons. The meeting.

Of course he knew what it was all about. He'd had to have been an idiot not to.

After the demotion to office jobs, then the removal of his security pass and clearance, and finally getting into work to find his name removed from the door to his office, and a brown envelope in his cubby hole requesting . . . no . . . demanding his immediate presence at his CEO's office.

The discussion had been . . . interesting . . . Nothing about his career or prospects. Nothing about his service. Nothing about how hard he had worked. Just a cursory thank you, and a note about retirement pension which would, of course, be paid with immediate effect.

He had tried to argue. He mentioned his friendship with Kate, daughter of the Brigadier, but that held no water. The Brigadier had vanished. Erased from the record even before the University Incident.

And Kate . . . well he had tried to call her several times over the last few months, but she never answered his calls. Any 'connection' he thought he had with her had turned out to be smoke and mirrors.

Thus, Captain Douglas Cavendish, fifteen years active service and experience. Enrolled when he was sixteen years old. Faithful to UNIT and its work . . . now thrown on the scrap heap.

What irked him most was that he really didn't know why. He'd not betrayed any secrets. Not spoken out of turn at parties. He had toed the UNIT line to the end.

The kettle started whistling, and he turned the heat off, pouring the boiling water into a cup containing two teabags and a splash of milk.

Two because that was the way a soldier took his tea. Like a navvy. Strong enough to stand the spoon up in! Strong like his mind and his backbone.

Strong enough to withstand anything that life or the universe threw at him.

He picked up the tea and blew it gently. He sipped it, wincing as it burned his lips. Still too hot.

He set it down on the counter and looked out the window. The sun was shining and slanting across the garden. Bees foraged for pollen around the flowers under the window. All was peaceful.

Cavendish headed back outside to the car and retrieved his bag. Just a few personal possessions taken from his grace and favour apartment in London.

The nearest village was half a mile away. A place called Devil's End, notorious among UNIT operatives as the site of one of their biggest achievements. The final capture of the Master in the seventies.

Never mind that the Church was blown to smithereens in the process.

He had been drawn to this cottage . . . buying it just seemed *right*. He liked the irony too, his hiding in the location of one of UNIT's legendary missions under the Brigadier. He never felt that it was strange that he started looking just after retrieving the book from the Black Archive. He never put two and two together that this was in fact the place that the book had been found, or that his compulsion to find somewhere safe to keep all his liberated treasures had started after he had taken the book.

Cavendish didn't think much about that at all. It was almost as though something was clouding his mind, making him feel wrapped in cotton wool whenever he tried to think harder about his actions and the rights and wrongs of stealing from his bosses.

All he knew was that he deserved the items.

Many years ago, while at school, he had read a vast, sprawling book called *Lord of the Rings* and in that book there was a character called Gollum. He had once been called Sméagol, but had coveted and wanted and desired a precious object, a ring, so badly that it had corrupted him to the extreme.

Cavendish sometimes thought that he might be like Gollum, coveting and protecting the precious things. But unlike that pitiable creature, he was not corrupted by them. Instead they gave him strength and hope.

Cavendish could feel the liberated tome even now, tugging at his mind.

He entered the cottage and went to the study, where the book was resting on the coffee table.

As he placed his hand on it, the cover seemed to glow gently with an amber light.

Cavendish smiled as a wave of good feeling flooded his body. He opened the covers and flicked through the first few pages.

The book opened on an image of a devil-like creature being taken up into the sky by a shaft of light. Cavendish had no idea what it meant.

As he looked at the page, the strange symbols there seemed to shift and move until they formed words which he felt he could read.

His lips started to move gently, as he tried the

unfamiliar word and letter sequences out.

Cavendish smiled to himself as that strange inner voice whispered that he was doing so well . . . that they were very pleased with him.

It never crossed his swaddled mind to wonder who 'they' were.

5
London 2586

A tall, scarred man wearing a heavy robe of office strode down a marbled corridor.

He entered into a palatial room where a woman was waiting for him.

The woman cocked her head gently. 'Grand Master', she said.

The man frowned at her. 'Thank you High Executioner,' he said sarcastically. 'What have you to report?'

The woman seemed unphased by his rudeness. She had long hair tied back, wore the uniform of a military officer, and exuded a sense of controlled power.

'I wanted to report . . . that we have located the remaining Time Channeller and Sensitive in 2050.'

The Grand Master nodded. 'So I hear,' he said. 'And then they escaped again. Your troops are ineffective.'

The High Executioner smiled. She pushed away from the table she had been leaning against and walked slowly around the room, the heels on her boots clacking against the polished marble floor.

'Indeed, but in escaping, they have been caught in another of my traps. My gargoyle chased them through London, to an area we had ensured was only occupied by one man. And that man had been hand-selected as he was originally from Nexus Point B.'

The Grand Master nodded. 'Nexus Point B . . . the village where the first Great Summoning was carried out.'

'Yes. Where our Lord Azal was summoned, and where the powers we now command were made public and available.'

'But what of these rogues? How can we dispose of them for good?'

'Even now,' said the High Executioner, 'some five hundred and eighty years ago, we have made contact with someone we can use. The plan has been afoot for several years, but now it reaches fruition.'

The Grand Master smiled, his face creasing into a toothy grin which made his scars twist into painful knots around his eyes.

The High Executioner nodded. 'Yes. And now we have reached the point of summoning once more. The power is growing in that timezone, and we can use that to destroy our final enemies.'

She slammed her hand down on the table.

'We *will* not be thwarted again. These meddling time travellers will be wiped out, and the Sodality's rule of past, present and future will be assured.'

The Grand Master moved across to the window, and looked out over the grey and blasted landscape which used to be London.

'Soon,' he whispered. 'Soon.'

6
Tea With Olive

Andy and Laura sat in Olive Hawthorne's cramped cottage while she fussed around them.

'Here you are, dear,' she said, giving Laura a cup and saucer.

'Thanks.'

'Biscuit?'

Laura selected one from the plate. It was chocolate and she had not enjoyed chocolate for a very long time.

As she munched on the biscuit, she studied Olive closely. She seemed to be in almost every aspect a typical old aged villager. Happy to bustle about and be everyone's friend and confidante.

But underneath the homely exterior was something more. A sense of great power, and a rod of iron that made her far more formidable than you might expect.

Her home too was dotted with strange and mystical items. On the dresser was a large clear globe of glass which exuded the same power. There were small pouches containing unknown ingredients, and other copper and iron images and shapes hung on the walls.

Despite all this, it felt safe. Indeed, far safer than she and Andy had felt for a long time. She was happy for the respite.

Olive sat opposite them in a saggy, stuffed armchair that had seen better days, but which fitted Olive like a glove.

The woman peered over her glasses at them. Studying them closely.

A cat wandered into the room, sniffed at their feet, and then leaped into Olive's lap where it sat, looking at the visitors with green slitted eyes.

'Don't mind Rhadamanthus,' said Olive, stroking the cat. 'He won't mind you.'

Olive looked at Andy and then Laura, and then back to Andy.

'Where are you from?' she asked.

Andy glanced at Laura. It was an insightful question.

'I . . . I'm not actually sure,' he began.

'And what about you?' Olive asked Laura.

Laura swallowed, not entirely certain how to answer.

Olive smiled at them both. 'You see, I can tell that you are not from around here. In fact, I'd go as far as to say that you are from a long way away. A *very* long way away.'

Andy smiled nervously. 'You could say that, yes.'

'I won't pry,' said Olive, 'I can sense that there is goodness in you both, and also pain. A lot of pain.'

Andy nodded.

Laura looked intently into her cup of tea and didn't answer.

'What is it that you need,' asked Olive gently.

Andy looked at her. 'I . . . I'm not sure,' he said. 'Maybe respite? Maybe some help of some sort, but I'm really not sure how you can help us.'

'Why don't you explain,' said Olive. 'Maybe in the telling, you can find the answer you seek. It often works.'

Andy exchanged a glance with Laura. 'I'm not sure you'd believe us,' he said.

Olive chuckled, a throaty laugh which filled the room.

'Oh,' she said when she could speak. 'Oh, I think you'll find that I'm more open minded than most.'

'Well,' said Andy. 'It all started about 600 years in the future . . .'

•   •   •   •   •

In that future, 583 years away, the High Executioner had assembled her team of acolytes.

They were standing in the nave of St Paul's Cathedral in London. This was one of the key locations for the Sodality as it had a history and a centre which made it ideal for these hunting parties.

The High Executioner closed her eyes and muttered an incantation under her breath. Alongside the acolytes one of the stone gargoyle creatures slowly stirred into life, its eye sockets glowing red as movement and sentience was bestowed to it.

The acolytes shifted nervously among themselves. Although they knew that these stone creatures were brought to life and controlled by the higher ministers in the Sodality, they were still terrifying to watch. As still as stone one moment, and then charging like some crazed bull the next.

Every one of those present had seen what the creatures could do. The weight of them could crush a man in an instant, and their horns were sharp and could pierce solid rock. Add to that a powerful force which allowed them to disintegrate solid matter with a gesture, and you had an impressive killing machine.

It was with creatures such as these that the Sodality had consolidated their power. No-one could stand against them.

When the gargoyle was fully activated, the High Executioner opened her eyes once more, surveying her team.

'We will send the creature through,' she said. 'It will locate the Channeller and his Sensitive companion and destroy them. It will also maintain the connection to that time for us, allowing us greater access to it. It is also where our secondary power source is located, and we need to ensure that this is boosted and maintained for as long as necessary.'

She checked her wrist on which was a chronometer. Rather than showing the actual time, however, this showed relative power levels. Time was not a concept that made much sense when you were talking about something happening 583 years ago in the same breath as 'today'.

She gestured to the ten acolytes who were gathered there.

'Two teams, now.'

The assembled group obediently split into two teams of five.

The High Executioner set one team chanting a particular set of cabbalistic words. This was designed to reach and influence their secondary power source, and to try to force open the window between the times even further.

While they moved in a tight circle, chanting continuously, the High Executioner prepared the second group. They were to send the gargoyle through when the moment arrived.

She consulted her wrist again, and noted that the power was low. It was almost as though her quarry were somewhere that was shielded, protected somehow.

Soon though . . . they could not remain hidden forever.

•   •   •   •   •

In his cottage, Cavendish felt the brush of a hand across his neck, and a feeling of happiness rested on him. He turned a page in the book, and saw that he could read the words written there.

His lips moved silently as the voice in his head congratulated and praised him the whole time.

He was doing a fantastic job. Everything was proceeding perfectly. All would be well.

He didn't notice that the sky was darkening outside, and that the birds and even the bees had deserted his bushes and flowers.

Silence was falling.

•   •   •   •   •

Andy stopped talking and drew a long breath. The story of how he and Laura came to be there was indeed incredible, but Olive had listened intently.

'So what do you think?' Andy asked. 'Have you any answers?'

Olive cleared her throat, and smiled gently again at them both.

'I think . . . I think your trials are coming to an end,' she said. 'And that you have the answer within you.'

Andy looked puzzled. 'But what does that mean?'

Olive sighed. 'I feel that you are among the last. This is why your enemies are so intent on finding you. But you have ended up here. This place contains so much power. Partly because of what has taken place here, but also partly because of the alignment of the leys, and the special position that we occupy in the mists of spacetime. I have seen such things . . . here the dead are never truly passed. I have seen spirits and phantoms. Things which would make your hair curl. Some of it can be explained, but most cannot.

'You, Andy, have a greater part yet to play, but you may not find it easy. And Laura, your future is hidden from me. I cannot tell.'

Laura looked at Andy in alarm. 'If I have no future . . . what does that mean?'

'Hush,' said Olive. 'What will be will be. None of us can change the past, but we can all change the future, regardless of where we originate.'

Rhad stretched on Olive's lap, and jumped down to the floor. 'Now, it is time,' said Olive sadly. 'You must go.'

She stood and ushered her guests out of the room.

'Remember that all things have their time. But that time sometimes is a flexible beast, and that not all things know how to behave within it.'

Andy shook Olive's hand. 'Thank you Miss Hawthorne,' he said. 'Telling you our story has been of help . . . I think.'

Laura agreed. 'Yes. I feel ... sort of ... calmer now.'

'That will be the tea,' chuckled Olive. 'Nothing like a nice cuppa to soothe the nerves.'

They stepped out of the cottage, and noticed that the sky was growing dark.

'There's a storm coming on,' noted Olive. 'I think you'd best get under cover as soon as you can. The pub should be open now.'

'We will,' said Laura. 'Thank you again Olive.'

They left the cottage and walked to the road.

Olive waved from her doorway, and the two friends walked back along the road, heading for the pub.

·   ·   ·   ·   ·

In 2586, the High Executioner felt the power suddenly rise as the window opened still further.

Good. Good. Exactly as she had planned.

'Start now,' she instructed the second group of acolytes, and they began their chant, moving slowly in a circle around the great stone beast which stood silently before them.

There was a noise like a rushing of air, and the dirt and leaves which littered the floor of St Paul's started to shift. Faster and faster they blew around the chanting acolytes until there was a maelstrom of power and wind buffeting them. Dust flew like smoke, and obscured the stone beast for a second, and when it cleared, the beast was no longer there.

The wind died slightly, but the acolytes knew better than to stop. They continued their circling chant, as the High Executioner smiled broadly.

Victory was hers.

7
The Attack

Andy and Laura heard it first as a faint rushing sound. Walking along the road in Devil's End, they could see that the sky was now black with clouds, and that a storm was approaching fast.

The wind picked up almost as though there was some elemental force playing with it. It buffeted them back and forth as they tried to walk.

'This doesn't look good,' said Laura. 'Do you think they have found us?'

There was a wailing howling noise, and ahead of them on the road, a stone gargoyle materialised from the winds. It lifted its great head with a grinding noise and sniffed, scenting the air.

Then it slowly turned until it was facing Andy and Laura.

They stood stock still in the wind and rain as it took one, and then another step towards them, the stone-on-stone grinding sound echoed above the sound of the howling wind.

'Run!' shouted Andy, and, grabbing Laura's hand, he turned and raced across the green towards the church. The stone beast gave chase, its hooves churning up the grass as it went.

Andy and Laura raced up into the small graveyard which dotted the lawns around the front of the church. There was nowhere to go.

The beast clattered up the steps, and stopped, watching them with its pinprick red eyes as they moved between the gravestones.

Andy spotted an exit from the churchyard, and, keeping firm hold of Laura's hand, ran for it.

The churchyard gave way to a narrow lane, and Andy and Laura ran down it, heading away from the village. Realising that they needed to find someone, anyone, whose time snake they could use to escape, they skidded to a halt and looked back. But return to the village was now blocked by the stone beast which cantered into view behind them.

They turned again and kept running.

Ahead of them, the path split, and they took the left hand route, which led down and around towards some wooded areas and fields.

As they ran, Andy wished that he had paid more attention to the time, and not spent quite so long with the woman, Olive.

They emerged after half a mile or so into a small clearing, beyond which could be seen a small cottage nestling in the woods. There were some ancient plinths in the clearing as well, like some sort of destroyed outhouse.

Andy dragged Laura behind the largest of the plinths and crouched down, panting heavily.

The place seemed strangely familiar to him, but he couldn't sense why.

Laura looked at him, she too was exhausted. 'How are we going to get away?' she asked.

Andy shook his head. 'No idea,' he said.

•   •   •   •   •

In the cottage, Cavendish felt a chill surround him. He looked up from the book that he had been reading. There was nothing there.

A small movement out in the hallway drew his attention. There seemed to be someone there!

As Cavendish watched, a man dressed in a silvery suit seemed to coalesce out of thin air. He had a balding pate and a neatly trimmed beard and moustache. He faded in and out like a badly tuned television set, and there was something else too. A buzzing sound, again like a radio signal on the edge of reception. The figure seemed to be trying to say something, but Cavendish could not make out the words.

Cavendish closed his eyes in terror.

. . . . .

In the clearing, Andy caught a glimpse of something across the other side. There seemed to be someone behind the trees there.

He looked closer, and realised that a man was standing there. The figure seemed to fade and Andy could clearly see the trees and brush through him.

He nudged Laura. 'Look!' he hissed.

Laura looked and drew in a gasp. 'It's . . . it's you!' she said.

Andy looked again. The figure was wearing the same silver suit as he was, and had the same beard and moustache.

At that moment there was a crash, and the stone gargoyle emerged from the undergrowth and stood by the side of the clearing. If it had been in any way a real animal, it would have been panting from the exertion of following the humans, but it was not, and the eerie silence and stillness was more unnerving than anything.

There was a gently grating noise as it swung its head back and forth, sensing the presence of the humans.

. . . . .

The High Executioner had her eyes closed. She was sensing the past through the channel opened by her acolytes, and connected to the gargoyle that they had sent back 583 years.

'There they are,' she whispered. 'I have you!'
She smiled a thin, cruel smile.
'Attack!'

•   •   •   •   •

At that moment, several things happened at once, though no one present knew or realised what the impact of them would be.

In the cottage, Cavendish cracked open his eyes to see that the ghostly presence had gone. He let out a whoosh of breath which steamed and hung in the air before him, and, realising that the great book was opened in front of him, closed it quickly.

Perhaps, he thought, this was the cause of the spiritual presence he had seen. It was icy cold though and he shivered. Maybe the heating had failed.

The closing of the book abruptly cut the channel of energy off that the great stone gargoyle had been using to maintain its vitalities and to supplement those coming from the future.

In the future, the High Executioner sensed the closing of the power source, and urged the gargoyle to attack before it was too late. The portal was still open.

In the clearing, the stone beast leaped onto one of the plinths beside Andy and Laura. The stone cracked and creaked from the weight, but held strong.

Laura threw her hands up in a reflexive gesture of defence, and Andy tried to shield her from the creature.

From the side, a ghostly shape also threw itself at the gargoyle, passing through the stone at the exact moment that Laura's hands touched the creature.

The portal activated, powered by the Time Channeller's own inner energy, and Andy and Laura found themselves no longer in the clearing, but in an echoey, smoke-filled chamber. There was chanting and movement all around them. The two humans looked at each other in terror, and then around themselves.

Andy could feel himself tearing, being pulled in many ways at once as the forces within the portal dragged part of his essence back and forth, maintaining his presence at the various nexus points that he and Laura had visited.

There was a blinding flash, and the two humans screamed as the acolytes bore down on them.

•   •   •   •   •

Silence.

In the clearing, nothing moved. The bulk of the giant stone gargoyle remained perched on the remains of the plinth. It was once more just a stone statue. The red of its eyes had faded, and now the worn stone glinted as the rain fell on it, pooled, and ran in rivulets down to the ground.

In the cottage, Cavendish sat slumped in his favourite armchair. In his hand was a rather overfull glass of whiskey. As he sipped the drink, his eyes were drawn to a photograph beside him on the table. One of a few he had decided to keep.

The man in the picture was military. You could tell from his uniform, his bearing, and even his eyes. This was an efficient military soldier.

Cavendish looked at the picture of his hero, Brigadier Alistair Gordon Lethbridge-Stewart, and sighed. The picture was old, probably taken during the Brigadier's heyday with UNIT in the seventies. But Cavendish was not thinking of the military, but of the Brigadier's daughter, Kate. He often thought of her. How she had caught his eye, how she moved, how she spoke... truth be told he was a little obsessed.

He took another sip of whiskey and let his eyes close. Maybe tomorrow he would try and contact her again. Maybe tomorrow. A small voice in the back of his head tried to raise an objection, but Cavendish quashed it with liquor.

•   •   •   •   •

In the far future, the High Executioner smiled as the bodies of the two humans were taken away.

Two less meddlesome time travellers for her to have to try and account for. She had no regrets over what she had done. She never did. Everything had a price, and her focus was on what the Sodality needed to do in order to gain the power from the ancient gods of this world.

She would brief the Grand Master, and they would plan for the next foray. Now that they had a potential power source *and* a gargoyle at one of the key nexus points, they would be able to take the next step.

All in all everything seemed to have worked out quite well for her.

PART TWO

1
The Cottage

Satanhall. Kate had never heard of it.

As the train hurried through the countryside, she looked again at the latest letter which had arrived with her.

It was from Douglas. Again. Probably the tenth such letter he had sent her. But this time was different. His handwriting was shaky and tentative, and the message pleading. *Please come!*

He had included a hand drawn map of the route from the station, but she hoped she might be able to jump in a taxi instead.

She looked out of the window and thought back to her first encounter with Douglas Cavendish. It had been at the University during the incident with the yeti and the web . . . strange enough to think about now.

That had been about eight years ago, and while she had subsequently gone on one 'date' with Douglas, it became obvious that he had been a career soldier, devoted to his job, but that following the incident, he was also very troubled. Trying to fit a relationship into all that was going to be hard work for both of them, and Kate wasn't sure she wanted to.

She knew this from her father. The famed Brigadier Lethbridge-Stewart. She loved him dearly, but he couldn't let the job go. If it wasn't manoeuvres in Scotland, it was strange sightings on the South Coast, or creatures seen in London housing estates . . . it was amazing that he had ever had time to be with a woman long enough for Kate herself to have seen the light of day.

But she had recognised a lot of her father in Douglas, and felt sorry for him. Via friends she had heard how he had become reclusive, almost hermit-like, and how this had affected his work to the point that UNIT had to let him go. He had moved from being top of the list of people you might choose for a mission, to being a liability who no-one wanted. Last chosen for the football team. That was Douglas.

So when the letters started arriving, Kate was sorry first, and then increasingly alarmed as he started to describe otherworldly happenings and incidents.

This culminated in this most recent letter, which seemed the most pained yet.

She really had little choice, and so left her own idyllic home: a houseboat on a lovely canal; and headed off to darkest Wiltshire, to a place she had never heard of to meet a man she barely knew who was in some sort of trouble. She just had to do this though. It was a compulsion, and she felt that she almost owed it to him to make sure he was okay.

Well, she was the Brigadier's daughter, and very good at looking after herself. Even her son Gordy looked up to her. Luckily, she had friends who could look after him, and so she was free for a long weekend and could go and check on Douglas. It was, she thought, just what her father would do if he knew that Douglas was in trouble.

Even so, it never occurred to her to contact her dad. Douglas had reached out to her, and she had to respond.

As the English countryside slipped past the windows, she closed her eyes and sunk back in her seat. She rarely travelled by train: everything she needed was within walking distance of her houseboat; and so this was a pleasure for her.

She only hoped that what awaited her at the end would also be pleasurable. Or at least that she could assess how Douglas was and arrange for professional help should he need it.

She sighed. Everyone's Mum. That was her. She just couldn't help herself.

•　　　•　　　•　　　•　　　•

The train pulled into Satanhall station and Kate grabbed her overnight bag and stepped off into the warm sunlight.

It was a beautiful October day. The skies were blue, and the sunshine was dappling the platform through the trees.

Kate headed for the exit, hoping that a taxi might be there. She had several notes stuffed in her purse for the trip should it be necessary.

At the front of the station, the road was empty. There were no cars, no traffic of any kind. She also noted that there were no other passengers.

A solitary platform guard pushed a broom along the platform at the far end.

Kate pulled the sheet of paper that Douglas had sent her from her pocket. She orientated it to the station, and with a sigh, set off along the road.

There were no houses, no people, no cars. If it wasn't for the tarmac she was walking on, then it could have been the middle ages!

After about five minutes walking, there was a smaller road off to the left. Kate consulted her paper. Yes, that seemed to be the way.

Didn't they believe in signs around here?

She set off down the smaller road, heading into a section overhung by trees. The scent of the country was strong: fresh grass and trees. She could hear pigeons cooing, and other birds too. The sun came through the trees in slanted rays which illuminated the insects and pollen in the air.

After a while, there was a track off the road. Again, no signs and no way of knowing where you were actually going. But according to Douglas' map, this was the way ...

Kate headed off down the track, opening a gate to pass through, and closing it again after herself. That was something you did in the country: close gates. Kate wasn't sure where she had heard that. Perhaps as a child? Or on television maybe.

She was really enjoying the walk though, helped by the sunshine and the sights, smells and sounds of the country. Whatever Douglas was doing here, it seemed to be a nice place to live. Especially if you wanted solitude.

Kate found that the rough dirt track on which she had been walking had given way to a muddy patch, with fields beyond. According to the map, the cottage where Douglas was staying was nearby. Kate spotted what seemed to be a clearer area up ahead, where the trees thinned a little, and she surmised that she might be able to spot the cottage if she got a little higher up.

She skirted the muddy patch, and made her way up to the clearing, hopping over a small ditch running through it.

As she entered the clearing, she noticed that it was quiet here. Much quieter than the woodlands she had been traversing. There seemed to be no birdsong at all. The silence was palpable.

She skirted a large bush, and stopped abruptly.

Right in front of her was a statue of some sort.

It was sitting/standing on a dais about four or five feet tall, and was like nothing she had seen before.

Made from some sort of marble or stone, it was festooned with ivy and moss as though it had been there a long time and nature was trying to reclaim it.

Kate approached and went round to the front of it. It was some sort of gargoyle she decided. Huge and ungainly, with two horns curling around its massive head, and two stubby arms tucked in at the sides.

Its feet ended in hooves, and they too were tucked underneath the statue, as though it were just crouching there on the plinth. Waiting.

Kate shuddered involuntarily, and decided that other peoples' ideas of decorative statues were not hers.

She set off again from the statue in a still uphill direction, hoping to spot the cottage. The way was crossed with brambles, and she had to tread carefully. She passed through some trees, alongside a patch of dense ferns, and then between a couple of bushes.

And found herself facing the statue again.

Kate shook her head and looked back the way she had come. Had she gone in a complete circle?

No. No she hadn't.

So was this another of the statues then? Perhaps the land owner liked the design and so had several installed.

Frowning, Kate passed the statue again, unnerved as the patches of moss and ivy growing on it seemed the same as before.

Keeping an eye on the statue, she headed in a different direction to the right . . . and momentarily stepped out again to find herself facing the statue again.

She was certain this time that she had not gone in a circle, and that this was the same place as she had been before—indeed the grass underfoot was crushed where she had walked. She could clearly see her two trails away from, and two coming towards the thing on the plinth.

There was a sudden sound from the bushes off to one side. A sound made all the more clear by the lack of any other noise in the clearing.

Kate looked intently around her.

'Hello? Anyone there?'

There was no answer. She thought she saw a movement off behind a tree, but when she looked more closely there was nothing there. A trick of the light perhaps.

She looked back at the statue. It seemed to be regarding her silently and balefully.

'Is this you?' she asked, hardly expecting a reply from a lump of stone.

'I don't need this. So I can't just leave, is that it?'

Unlike many people, Kate had grown up with stories of the fantastic from her father, and she had a healthy respect for anything which seemed to be *not right*. And this whole situation reeked of *not right* to her.

She reached into her pocket and pulled out her mobile phone. Keeping her eyes on the statue, she punched a familiar 'favourites' button and held the phone to her ear. There was a crackling sound as though it had been answered.

'Hello? Dad?'

The crackling continued. Kate checked the screen. No signal. The phone was as good as useless.

She put it back in her pocket and looked again at the huge statue.

As she stared at it, she considered that the statue seemed to be looking back at her. A feeling crept over her that this was not just a statue, but that this was something more. Something real and dangerous.

But it was just stone wasn't it?

There was something about the statue that she couldn't put her finger on. A sensation like pins and needles in her scalp which made the hairs on the back of her neck stand up.

She reached out with one hand, and as it approached the foot of the statue, so the hairs on her arms stood up as though there was a static electric field all around her.

'There's *something*,' she muttered, touching the cold stone foot of the creature with her hand.

•   •   •   •   •

Kate was suddenly somewhere else.

The air was different, sweeter with the smell of incense and smoke. The light was tinged with red, and underfoot she could feel dust and rubble rather than grass.

She could hear chanting: guttural and alien. Words and phrases which had no meaning hung in the air around her.

She turned on the spot, not quite knowing or understanding what had happened. Her arm was outstretched, and she pulled it back into her body.

There seemed to be people coming closer around her. Shadowy figures in cowls which hid their faces moving in a circle.

She turned again, twisting, and...

•   •   •   •   •

... and was back in front of the statue in the clearing. She drew a huge breath into her lungs. She could still smell and taste the incense.

She looked at her hand and arm and saw that the fine hairs were still standing on end. She shook her arm. That was not something she wanted to repeat.

She looked out away from the statue, and suddenly, through the swaying trees, saw what she had been looking for: a cottage.

With a backwards glance at the statue, still standing, impassively in place, Kate headed towards the cottage. Hopefully this time she would be allowed to get there!

•   •   •   •   •

The High Executioner strode into one of the sub-rooms of St Paul's Cathedral, her eyes were bright and she was waiting for some good news for once.

Since the two time travellers had been destroyed, things had quietened, but she had ordered that a monitor be maintained on the time zone: key nexus that it was.

Through her acolytes, and the partial portal maintained by the stone gargoyle, she had been able to insinuate herself into the mind of the one known as Cavendish. He had proven to be of great value, providing the energy that they needed to maintain the connection.

In the centre of the lower room was a large throne-like chair, and seated in that chair was the acolyte chosen to be the voice of the Sodality in Cavendish's mind.

The man was a physical wreck. The High Executioner had ordered that anything other than the mind be excised from the acolyte so that he could fully focus on the task at hand. Thus his body was withered and decaying. Leather straps prevented the blood from circulating fully, causing his limbs to atrophy, blacken and eventually die.

His head was held in a copper cradle to keep it upright, and a network of pipes and valves brought water and nutrients to the brain.

The High Executioner inspected her creation. They had come a long way since the experiments which created hideous machine-creatures. This was the current cycle of progress, allowing the mind to be freed to maintain the psyonic connections far longer than any 'normal' human could bear.

She leaned close to the creature in the chair.

'I need connection,' she hissed. 'Now.'

The shattered man moaned, but obeyed his mistress. The acolytes surrounding them increased their chanting, and the High Executioner prepared to determine exactly who this stranger was that had travelled via the portal. Who had been able to breach their own defences and enter their headquarters with no prior warning.

This was something that could not be permitted.

2
Cavendish

Kate found that the path from the statue wound around and led to a small gate. It was very picturesque, and she took a moment to look around.

There was even an ancient well just outside the gate. She went to it and peered in.

It descended into darkness, and she noted that the bucket was missing. *Not much use as a well now,* she thought.

Kate opened the gate and stepped into the garden. The strange silence lifted, and she could hear birdsong again, and the buzzing of insects.

The cottage sat nestled in nature as though it had always been there. There were flowers all around it, and the lawn, although a little long, showed signs of having been tended at some point.

'Kate!'

The voice and a grimy hand on her arm made her jump. She stepped back and turned to see the dishevelled form of Captain Cavendish. He had stepped out of the foliage behind her.

Cavendish was wearing what might once have been a smart suit, but now it was crumpled and dirty. He was unshaven and the stubble and beard growth suggested that this was for some time.

It looked like he hadn't changed his clothes too.

'Thank goodness you came,' Douglas blurted, his eyes flicking back and forth and all around.

· · · · ·

To be honest to himself, Cavendish had never expected

Kate to actually come. Yes, he had written to her many times, but for her to actually be there...

Plus there was the uncertainty of his perception. He did keep seeing things that didn't seem to be there. And hear them too.

He checked all around, but she was there, and real.

Kate looked at him. 'Douglas?'

Almost immediately the voice in Cavendish's head chimed in. To Cavendish it was cold and controlled. An echo of what his own voice used to sound like.

'She knows him!'

·   ·   ·   ·   ·

In the far future, the shattered semblance of a man spoke in the same cold tones.

'She knows him!'

The High Executioner smiled. The link was sound, and they were still in control.

'Tell me everything,' she said, and nodded to the acolytes to keep the psyonic link active.

·   ·   ·   ·   ·

Kate's voice echoed back to Cavendish as though from a long distance away. These 'episodes' were getting worse...

'Douglas? It's me, Kate? You wrote to me?'

Cavendish shrugged, more of a tic, and looked around again. 'Glad I got you. Phones not working. Nearest post office miles away. Had to walk. Transport up the creek.'

Kate looked at the man closely. He was exhibiting many symptoms which she recognised as being some form of shell shock. Recovery trauma from the events that he had been forced to confront perhaps? She had seen this several times before in friends of her dad.

She kept her voice gentle, feeling that this was the best way to connect with Douglas, who was obviously feeling the strain.

'What... what's been happening?'

She looked at him again and realised why he looked so ragged and grimy.

'Have you been sleeping rough?'

Cavendish twitched at the cottage, then back to her.

'Had to. Couldn't stay in the cottage. Too much happening. Too much going on.'

Cavendish winced as the calm voice in his head said: 'Get her away from here.'

'I can't,' he replied. 'Need her.'

'Get a grip, man,' said the cold voice.

To Kate, this exchange was bewildering. Douglas seemed to be talking to himself.

Cavendish took a deep breath.

'I... I'm sorry... a lot has been happening... I'm finding it hard to cope. I get confused on my own. Not sure who I am. There are... voices... voices in my head...'

'I'm not sure I know who you are either,' said Kate. 'Why did you ask me to come here? You said it was something to do with dad...'

Cavendish looked at his feet. 'You were the only person who might understand.'

Kate's eyes widened. 'Understand?'

Cavendish nodded and started to wander back towards the cottage.

Kate followed him. 'But you nearly killed us all? Everything...'

Cavendish's mind again flashed back to the events at the University. He had indeed made some mistakes.

'I know... I know...'

'So why should I trust you?' Kate asked. 'What's this got to do with dad?'

Cavendish turned and took her hand. 'You were the only one who visited me, Kate. The only one who cared. When it was all over... when I was taken to... to... hospital. Severe mental and nervous burn out. Nothing left. But you . . .'

Kate looked into his eyes. So much pain. 'Dad told me you had been a good friend to him. Before. I felt I owed him that.'

'But you were there! You saw . . .'

'I know. I wouldn't have believed it if I hadn't been . . . and dad said he had seen much, much worse in his time . . . but, Douglas, you were discharged. No blemish on your record. None of it was your fault . . .'

Cavendish sighed again. 'Burn out. That's what they called it. Fine young officer. Prime of life. Excellent UNIT material . . . and then just put out to roost. No regard for what I wanted. They said I was finished.'

The voice in Cavendish's head said in a slow, gloating manner, 'Not finished yet.'

Cavendish shook his head in a nervous tic. 'Kate. You came. I didn't think you would. You'll help me? Help me sort it before anyone finds out?'

'Of course I will . . . if I can . . .'

Kate looked at Cavendish again. His eyes were pleading and she could see there was no malice in the man.

'You'd have said anything to get me to come, wouldn't you?' Kate dropped his hand and looked around. 'Look . . . I've just walked miles from the station. It's the end of October . . . I'm tired . . . I'm cold . . . my feet hurt and I'm dying for a cup of tea.'

She glanced back the way she had come into the garden. 'And that clearing . . . back there in the woods? I saw someone, I'm sure I did. Something happened and . . . silly really, but every path I took lead back to the statue . . .'

Cavendish looked agitated at mention of the statue. He clasped his hands to his upper arms and hugged himself.

In his mind the cold voice chuckled. 'We know all about the statue . . .'

'Don't want to go there,' he blurted.

Kate's eyes narrowed. 'Why?'

'It . . . it's not safe.'

Kate looked at the way back to the statue, to Cavendish and finally to the cottage.

'Well if you'd rather go to the cottage . . .'

This dilemma confused Cavendish and he looked frantically from Kate to the cottage and back. His eyes large and pleading.

Kate took pity on him. 'Tell you what, let's look at the statue first, and then I'll make you a nice cup of tea . . . How does that sound?'

With that, she took Cavendish's arm and gently led him back to the gate and the path that led to the statue.

There was definitely something going on here, and she hoped she could get Douglas to tell her what it was before the man broke completely. He seemed permanently on the edge, and her heart went out to him. No-one should have to live like that.

3
The Statue

As Kate and Cavendish rounded the bushes, the sight of the statue sitting there on its plinth was as disturbing as ever.

Cavendish pulled away from Kate and stood watching the thing intently, as if at any moment it was going to rear up and pounce on them both.

Kate cautiously approached the thing. As before it seemed to suck the energy from the clearing.

She lifted her hand and held it close to the stone. She could feel the strange tingling sensation, and there was the slight smell of ozone in the air also.

'Something happened when I touched it before,' said Kate. 'What do you know about it?'

Cavendish retreated further into himself. 'Nothing,' he said a little too quickly. 'Nothing at all.'

Cavendish looked around at the clearing. The light was starting to fade, and the area was as silent as the grave.

'We'd best get back,' he said. 'Dark soon.'

Kate nodded, regarding the statue with suspicious eyes. 'Well... there's nowhere else to go...'

She dropped her hand and returned to where Cavendish was standing.

'Come on then,' she said brightly.

Then she turned and headed back towards the cottage. Cavendish stayed looking at the statue for a moment longer, then he scuttled after her.

In the clearing, the silence was deafening. As the light slowly faded, so a strange white mist started to pool around the base of the statue.

4
Lost in Time

Andy opened his eyes. He felt odd, as though he had been sleeping on his arm, and it had all gone pins and needles and numb. Except that it was his whole body.

He looked down at his hands. They were there. And he was wearing his favourite silvery suit.

His legs and feet seemed to be there as well.

But where was he?

He looked around. He seemed to be back on Earth, in Devil's End, at the place that he and Laura . . . that he and Laura . . . he couldn't quite place the thought. Something had happened. They had been caught. Dragged back through time to the Sodality's future. But there, the intense pressures of the time vortex, and the powerful connection that the Sodality were maintaining back to this time . . . was he alive?

Andy concentrated for a moment. He could sense a channel nearby, and he found that he was able to draw a little of the power from it.

He looked at his hands and they faded from view momentarily before solidifying into what looked like real flesh.

He remembered the tearing sensation as the Sodality tried to destroy him. It appeared they only partially succeeded, and now he was in this ghost-like form, separated from his body, and thrown back to this key nexus point.

If he focussed, he could see all times laid out before him. Perhaps this was his own time snake. He could see places he had been, battles he had fought, and he felt that he could step into them, perhaps to relive them, perhaps to influence them.

More importantly was the fact that he was in this place at this time. An event of clear importance to the Sodality was about to take place, and he was right in the line of fire so to speak.

The problem was, what to do?

Andy tried heading to the cottage. Perhaps if he could talk to Cavendish, to warn him.

Cavendish? Who was Cavendish?

Andy realised that past, present and future were all accessible to him. He knew what was going to happen, he just had no clue as to how to stop it. He knew who Cavendish was, what he had done, what he was going to do...

He had never felt so helpless.

Andy slipped through the cracks in now and found himself at the clearing where Kate Lethbridge-Stewart was about to arrive.

There was a movement in the bushes, and she stepped out, looking concerned.

Andy drew some power from the portal, and his foot cracked against a stick on the ground. The extent to which he could influence his surroundings was limited.

'Hello? Anyone there?'

Kate called out and looked around. At one point she looked directly at Andy, but didn't see him.

'Is this you?' she asked the statue. 'I don't need this. So I can't just leave, is that it?'

While she pulled out her mobile phone—an object long obsolete in Andy's time, but which he recognised the function of at an intellectual level, and indeed had seen himself during his many trips to this time—Andy crept back around the clearing. He knew what was going to happen here and had to ensure he protected Kate from the worst.

She put the phone away and reached out to touch the statue. This was it.

As Andy watched, her hand connected with the foot of the gargoyle, Kate's image flickered and she vanished.

Andy concentrated on her time snake, and poured a little energy into it. Seconds later, Kate reappeared, looking puzzled and shocked but none the worse for wear.

Andy could sense the confusion and fury of the Sodality in the far future, and smiled to himself.

At least she was safe, and if he could help keep her that way, then maybe they could prevent the coming events from being the end of everything.

Andy phased out of solidity again. He had to try and keep his mind on the order that things needed to play out. Something that was hard enough even when you had all your corporeal parts intact. As an insubstantial ghost, it was even harder!

5
Tea with Douglas

'... if you think I'm staying outside, then you're sadly mistaken!'

Kate put her hands on her hips and looked at Douglas in amazement.

'But we can't stay inside ... it's ... it's dark and ...' his voice started to tail off, so Kate interrupted him.

'... and you can stop that right now! There's nothing to be scared of. Look, you asked me to come here, right?'

Douglas looked at her, wide eyed and terrified, and after a moment he nodded.

Kate considered that this was like dealing with her son ... she needed to be calmer, more reasoned.

She smiled at him gently. 'And now I'm here. I've got no choice but to stay, so let's go and see what's got you so upset, eh?'

Douglas nodded.

'It's all right. Honestly it is. We can't make tea out here now can we?'

Kate's logic was impeccable, but she was very concerned about him. His behaviour was very unpredictable and for the first time in her life, she didn't feel certain about her circumstances. What was really going on with Douglas? Was he losing his mind?

'Douglas? Douglas? Should I try and call for someone?'

Cavendish shook his head. 'No ... no ...'

Kate pressed on: 'There's a Doctor I know ...'

'I'm fine. Really.'

With that, Cavendish seemed to relax a little, even offering a slight smile to Kate.

Kate nodded, turned, and entered the cottage.

Cavendish, as usual, cast a glance around himself and then followed her inside.

·　　·　　·　　·　　·

The cottage was quiet.

A grandfather clock clicked away the seconds at the end of the hallway. But there was no other sound or movement.

Kate and Cavendish stood in the hallway and waited.

Kate had no idea why Cavendish was so upset. It could be anything, and her nerves were jangling now too. This whole situation was very odd and she couldn't stop herself from wondering exactly what had happened outside with the gargoyle.

She put her rucksack down on the floor and looked up the stairs. There was a nice stained glass window at the top, and the fading sun was glinting through it.

To her left were a couple of steps down into a dining room. She looked in.

There was nothing to see. A dark wooden table was set with knives and forks as if ready for dinner. Nothing seemed out of place.

Kate's eyes scanned the room, skipping right over the faint figure of Andy who was standing in full view watching them intently.

'Nothing,' said Kate.

She moved down the hallway. A little further on was a closed door leading to the understairs area. She tried the door but it was locked.

Cavendish took a couple of steps towards her and placed his hand on the door, as though ensuring that it was indeed closed and secure.

'Yes. Keeps him at bay.'

His eyes scanned the hallway before coming to rest on Kate. He leaned forward as though imparting a big secret. 'But sometimes he comes out.'

Cavendish suddenly heard the cold voice in his head once more. 'It will be opened soon.'

'No,' he retorted to the air. 'It must stay locked!'

Kate was looking at Cavendish. 'Keeps who at bay? Why must it stay locked?'

Cavendish looked surprised, as though he hadn't meant to say those words out loud. 'There's . . . a person . . . a figure . . . I don't know. Honestly.'

Kate looked at Cavendish for a moment and then headed upstairs.

When she had gone, Cavendish tried the door handle again, just to make sure that it was indeed locked. He then put his ear to the door and listened, before once more trying the handle.

With this ritual complete, Cavendish was happy.

Kate returned from upstairs. 'Nothing up there either . . . Whatever it is that's going on in this house, it's being pretty quiet about it.'

Behind her, on the stairs, the silent hard-to-see figure of Andy stood, watching.

Cavendish shrugged.

'Are you *sure* you're all right?' asked Kate. 'It *is* a bit cut off out here, and you're only just out of hospital. At least let me call for a doctor.'

She pulled her mobile phone from her pocket again and checked the screen. Still no signal.

'Hopeless,' she said under her breath, and moved past Cavendish into the front parlour of the house. There she sat on the overstuffed sofa, and regarded Cavendish with a critical eye.

Cavendish stood by the doorway, not quite sure what he should do. It had been a long time since he had entertained anyone.

Drinks. That's what people did. Normal people. They offered each other drinks.

Cavendish went to the cabinet on which stood the photograph of the Brigadier. He pulled out two glasses, and a bottle of Scotch, then sat in his favourite chair.

'You're going to have to open up a little, Douglas,' said Kate. 'As far as I can see, this is a perfectly normal cottage, but with some heating issues, and a little dry rot in the walls...'

'I wasn't sure you'd believe me,' said Cavendish, pouring two generous shots of the Scotch into the glasses.

'I came didn't I? I'm not in the habit of dropping everything to run off somewhere, you know. You're lucky that Beth was available to look after Gordy...'

Cavendish looked up at Kate. 'Gordy?'

'... my son? Otherwise I'd not have been able to come.'

'I am grateful,' said Cavendish, passing her one of the glasses.

There was a pause while Cavendish and Kate sipped their drinks. Cavendish's eyes flitted all around the room and the doorway, while Kate studied Cavendish intently.

After a moment, Kate placed her glass down on the table, noting the large leather-bound tome there, as well as a manila folder stamped with the familiar UNIT decal, the words TOP SECRET and the code number '05-06/71 JJJ' stencilled on the front. She decided to make no comment.

Cavendish cleared his throat. 'I think . . . I think this place is haunted.'

Kate looked up sharply. 'By this person you've been seeing?'

Cavendish swallowed and nodded.

'Douglas,' said Kate gently, 'You're a UNIT operative...'

'*Ex*-UNIT operative...'

'Okay, *Ex*-UNIT operative . . . and you're telling me you're afraid of the ghost of Aunt Mable?'

Cavendish looked at his hands. 'It's not as simple as that.'

'I should hope not,' said Kate.

'I've seen things in this place at night,' Cavendish said. 'Heard things too. Crying and screaming. Souls in torment.'

Kate narrowed her eyes. *Souls in torment.* She remembered what had happened when she had touched that statue. Where it had taken her (or what it had shown her): exactly what had happened was not clear to her.

Cavendish continued: 'At first I thought it was the drink—after I was discharged from the hospital, I hit the bottle quite hard. Trauma can do that to a chap, they say. But when the voices started, I gave it up, but it wasn't the booze at all. By then it was too late...'

He reached out and touched the large book, stroking his fingers over it almost reverentially.

'What's that?' Kate asked.

Without waiting for an invitation, she pulled the book over to her and opened the cover. Pictures of a devil-like creature were revealed. She flicked on a few more pages: more images of death and destruction, devils and mayhem. She looked too at the words printed in the book, but then found that she could not focus on them. They kept shifting around, making themselves hard to read.

'Devils, demons and spells?' she said, raising her eyes to look once more at Cavendish.

He squirmed in his seat, but then seemed to gain resolve. He looked at Kate.

'It was meant to be my pension. UNIT looks after its own... they said. Only while you're useful to them.'

Kate considered that. Her father had always said that UNIT was a great place to serve as they always looked after their fellows.

'But dad always said—'

'—It's fine for your father!' Cavendish almost spat the words. 'Brigadier Alistair Gordon Lethbridge-Stewart gets a *much* better deal. But for an unknown Captain... forget it!'

Cavendish pulled the book in front of him once more, and stroked the pages with his fingers as his mind went back in time. 'I once asked your father if he had ever taken any "keepsakes" from his time with the Taskforce... the irony is I did just the same.'

Kate frowned. 'I was as surprised as anyone when we found that he had... Sorry... go on.'

Cavendish almost ignored her, so intent was he on his own memories and story.

'UNIT has a secure facility. Just outside London. Vast warehouse-like place, covered with alarms and barbed wire. They keep all their "treasures" in there. Strange alien objects ... guns ... pieces of equipment ... crates of shop dummies ...'

Kate smiled. 'Why would they keep crates of shop dummies ...?'

Cavendish ignored her.

'Chipper Norris, an old friend from Oxford, was really into old parchments and manuscripts. Worth a fortune he once told me, so I took it.

'You stole it?'

'It was quite easy, really, just slipped it under my jacket and walked out with it. No-one questioned VO staff, security getting a bit lax and all that.'

'But what's it for?' asked Kate.

'For? It was a means. A way out. Something I wanted. After I took it, I kept it hidden for months. Then, after my ... my ...' Cavendish shuddered and slumped back in his chair. Kate stayed silent, and after a moment, Cavendish straightened his back and continued.

'When I first tried to read it, I couldn't make any sense of the words, they all kept jumping and moving. But then, I found I could read sections. Strange words, poetic ...'

Kate looked down at the book and back at Cavendish. 'So you've been reading from the book?'

Cavendish nodded.

'And that's when things started to happen to you?'

'I thought I could control it. I thought it would be a way for me to get some power, some respect. To *be* someone. But it started to read itself. To control me!'

Cavendish reached for his drink, and the cool, cold voice echoed in his head once more.

'But not totally in control. We need more power, the final incantations ...'

Cavendish blinked and with a shaking hand placed the

glass back on the table.

'Which is when I started to hear voices in my head, to see things ... people ... Kate ... I ... I ...'

Cavendish broke down in tears, and Kate moved to sit on the arm of his chair, stroking his matted hair. There wasn't much more she could do.

She moved the book away from his hands and closed the cover.

'Maybe we need that tea now ... leave that book alone.'

Cavendish sniffed and composed himself. 'I intend to. But you'll see, Kate. You'll see what we're up against.'

Kate stood. 'We?' she said, and headed off to find the kitchen and to make them both a cup of tea.

Left alone with his thoughts Cavendish worried that he had brought Kate into this. Deep down he knew he was in serious trouble. He needed help and so had been compelled to contact Kate even though UNIT should have been his first port of call. The problem there was he had broken the law by removing his trophies from the vault. He couldn't call in for help, and if he did, would anyone even believe him?

No, Kate had been the only person he could reach out to. He knew that, just as surely as he realised he had feelings for her. It was all too complicated. But if anyone could help him straighten out, she could.

Kate returned with the tea and they sat drinking in silence. The hot liquid revived Cavendish for a short time, making him feel stronger, more stiff upper lipped, in the way that only a strong cuppa could.

'Thank you,' he said.

'What for?' Kate asked.

'For coming when I needed you.'

6
Night Terrors

'You can sleep here,' said Cavendish, showing Kate into a neat bedroom.

'Are you sure you'll be alright,' she asked, concerned.

'I'll be fine,' he assured her. 'Just fine.'

Kate looked around the room, everything seemed completely normal. 'Okay then. But just shout if you need me. If anything happens?'

Cavendish nodded and backed out the room, closing the door behind him.

Kate looked around the room again, and sat on the bed. She pushed off her shoes and lay back on the bed.

Her mind was going six to the dozen, turning over the stories she had heard today, and the unusual events she had witnessed.

Douglas' behaviour was odd, but he didn't seem dangerous. He was terrified of something and Kate wanted to get to the bottom of it if she could.

Something was going on here . . . she just wasn't sure quite what.

What of *that* book? Kate had felt nothing when she touched it, but Douglas' attachment to it concerned her. He had caressed it as though he drew some comfort from it. But then how strange to say it was 'reading itself'. What did it all mean?

•   •   •   •   •

Having shown Kate to her room, Cavendish made his way back downstairs in the cottage. He had a vague idea about washing up the cups and glasses and then getting some sleep himself.

Half way down the stairs, however, he paused. Something felt wrong. There was a sensation . . . a feeling . . . and he had felt this way before.

'Oh no,' he mumbled. 'Not again!'

•   •   •   •   •

The sky growled over St Paul's Cathedral, and the grey dust clouds swirled and flickered with lightning.

In the grime and grit of a devastated London, three large stone gargoyles prowled, looking for anything they could devour. Most humans were now dead or hiding so securely that even the most devious of promises from the High Executioner could not tempt them out.

So the stone creatures remained alert, hunting for anything they could call prey.

Within the Cathedral, there was a frantic scurrying as one of the acolytes, a woman who had once been called Eva, hurried to fetch the High Executioner.

She gained access to her rooms, and now waited for her to join her. After a moment, the imperious High Executioner, in command of the Sodality, swept out of her chambers and down to where the link with 2003 was being maintained.

She was wearing her usual leather trousers tucked into high boots, with a flowing silk top. Eva knew that the top disguised the fact that she wore knife holsters on each arm, and that she had a sharp sword clipped to one leg. There was no way that she was going to be caught out.

As they approached the chair upon which the remains of the man maintaining contact with Cavendish were placed, one of the other acolytes scurried forward.

'Madame,' he began. 'We feel it has started.'

The High Executioner frowned. What had started?

Nothing started without her saying so.

The creature in the copper harness rolled its eyes to look at the High Executioner.

'The portal is being forced open,' he said calmly. 'More power is needed. It may be time to take the next move and to secure this nexus point.'

The High Executioner nodded, and gestured for Eva to attend her.

'We need ten more acolytes here now,' she said. 'Go!'

Eva ran off to chase down more people to keep the strange powerful chanting going. Those who had been doing this were now exhausted, herself included.

While she did this, the High Executioner turned her attention to the man in the machine.

'What can you see?'

The man closed his eyes and murmured, 'More power...'

The acolytes surrounding them, although tired, started up the usual power chant, bringing the strange psyonic science to life through their words.

'Excellent, excellent,' said the calm voice of the creature. 'We have connection. We can begin.'

'Keep it going,' said the High Executioner. 'I want to control this zone... I *have* to control this zone!'

'Time for a bedtime story,' said the creature on the chair.

•   •   •   •   •

On the stairs in the cottage, Cavendish paused. He could feel the voices in his head.

'Time for a bedtime story.'

Cavendish shook his head. 'No, no!'

He suddenly realised what these voices wanted and started to struggle mentally. 'No. Kate's here to help!'

'You invited the woman here because you think she likes you,' taunted the voice. 'And you certainly like her.'

'No!'

'I know you better than that. So we can use her to get what we want . . .'

Cavendish put his hands to his head, struggling in agony. 'I won't . . . I won't.'

The voice came in a harsh whisper: 'You can't stop us!'

Cavendish suddenly stopped struggling and brought his hands down from his face. His face was calm, and his eyes glinted with a malign intelligence. He looked over to where Kate's room was, and a slow, cruel smile spread across his lips.

Silently, he continued his way down the stairs and into the living room. There he picked up the large leather book and laid it on the table in front of him.

He opened it to a certain page, ran his finger down the page, and began to read: '*Snubs sorc toh ynnepa owt ynnepa eno snubs sorc toh snubs sorc toh.*'

·   ·   ·   ·   ·

The surge of power as Cavendish, now controlled by the Sodality, opened the portal still further, took the High Executioner by surprise.

Rivulets of blue electricity started to run around the copper cradle containing the human conduit in her time, and the chanting acolytes seemed to gain in power and confidence.

She paced back and forth, delighted at the progress. Soon the power would be hers and hers alone. She could sense it.

·   ·   ·   ·   ·

Lying on the bed in the cottage, Kate felt a change in the air. As though someone had let a fresh blast of sea air into the house. She looked over at the window and thought she saw something moving.

Kate pushed herself off the bed and went over to look out. There was nothing to see but darkness. She shrugged, wondering if Douglas' instability was contagious.

. . . . .

Outside in the forest clearing, the hunched stone statue was wreathed in white mist. The forest was silent. No animals or birds would have dared to be out on this night. They could sense the power in the air.

. . . . .

Cavendish, controlled by his future masters, continued to read from the book: *'Regna meh tot emoc emoc emoc!'*

. . . . .

Outside, the mist covered statue quivered as though some shockwave travelled through it from the ground. The mists swirled around it, obscuring it from sight.

There was a curious grinding sound. Of stone on stone. Of great marble objects clashing against each other.

The mists swirled, and when they cleared, the statue had gone.

Nothing remained but the plinth on which it had stood.

. . . . .

In her room, Kate peered intently out of her window. She was sure she had seen something out there.

She moved her face close, seeing her own reflection looking back at her.

Perhaps that was it? She had seen her own reflection?

There was a sudden bang on her bedroom door.

Kate launched herself away from the window, on alert as something moved outside in the hallway.

What she didn't see was that her reflection in the glass *remained there*! The mirror image of Kate was still looking in through the window!

Kate moved to the door. Strange white mist rolled under it.

She put out her hand to the handle, and felt the same static electric shocks run up her arm, bringing the hairs upright once more.

She gently pulled the handle and opened the door.

•   •   •   •   •

Outside the room, in the upper hallway, all was dark. Tendrils of white mist flowed around the floor, however.

Kate moved to the top of the stairs and carefully made her way down in the darkness. There was nothing to see except the mist which, when it touched her ankles, was ice cold.

Kate noted that the mist seemed to be coming from underneath the locked understairs doorway, but aside from this there was nothing untoward about the house.

In the room opposite the locked door, Cavendish sat at the table, his head in his hands, and the book in front of him.

As Kate approached he looked up, and his face was white.

'Douglas?' she said.

He blinked and some semblance of life seemed to flow back into him.

'I'm sorry . . . I'm so sorry. The voices . . . they took control again, completed the incantation. Now they have enough power to start the next stage . . .'

Cavendish struggled to stand, and Kate helped him up. There was obviously something very wrong here.

They moved to the hallway which was icy cold. Kate

noticed that her breath steamed as she breathed.

This was like a million supposed haunted houses that those shows on television visited.

Suddenly, there was a movement in the hallway ahead of them, and before Kate's eyes the figure of a man materialised from nowhere. He was dressed in a smart but futuristic looking silver suit, he had a bald pate, but a neatly trimmed moustache and beard. He seemed to be talking to them, but no sound could be heard.

He gesticulated in frustration and again could be seen mouthing silently.

Kate realised that her own mouth was gaping open.

'He's back,' whispered Cavendish, stepping backwards down the hall.

The see-through man stepped towards them, still trying to make himself understood. He gestured to the locked door, and then stepped right through it, vanishing from sight.

Kate realised she was holding her breath, and let it out in a rush.

'What . . . was that?' she asked.

'A ghost? You saw him too? I *knew* it wasn't just me . . .'

'But I don't believe in ghosts . . .'

Kate tried the understairs door again but it was locked.

'There's no way he could have got through here . . . unless there's a secret opening . . .'

Kate started to feel and press around the door, in the hope of finding some sort of hidden catch or something, but there was nothing.

'There's no point,' said Cavendish. 'There is no hidden door. I did the same thing the first time I saw him.'

'But people can't just walk through walls. It's not . . .'

'. . . human?'

'Why do you say that?' asked Kate. 'I was thinking "natural". What was that you said about them having enough power. Who are "they"?'

'I'm not sure.' Cavendish sighed. 'I think they're from another place . . . maybe another time. They promised me power if I'd help them. At first I was sceptical, but working with UNIT gives you . . . insights . . . into what's going on.'

'I could have guessed. Why did you say that this . . . this ghost thing . . . was not human?'

'In UNIT's secure facility I saw the files. Everything neatly labelled and locked away as if that would help control it.'

Cavendish seemed to make a decision.

'I must show you.' He grabbed Kate's hand and started off down the hallway to the front door.

'Come,' he said. 'Come see.'

7
The Collection

Cavendish led Kate out of the house into the night air. They followed a path that wound around the side to behind the cottage, and down a short driveway to a garage.

He seemed to have regained much of his strength, and he chattered away as they walked.

'... you do know Kate, we're not alone here. Earth has been visited many, many times, but UNIT hushes it up. The things I saw ... photographs ... witness reports ... crates of equipment like something out of a science fiction film ... and then there's the specimens.'

'Specimens? They have real live aliens?'

'Not live ... not that I saw anyway ... but one of the vaults is floor to ceiling with bell jars and other glass containers. Some of the things there—tentacles, lumps of flesh, foetuses, alien shapes and forms all sitting silently in formaldehyde ...'

Kate remembered a news report she had seen about an artist who pickled creatures for art.

'What? Like Damien Hurst?'

They had reached the door to the garage, and Cavendish opened it, standing back to let Kate enter first. 'Take a look,' he said.

Kate stepped cautiously into the garage. Cavendish flicked on a light and a dim bulb lit the interior.

It was full of shelves, no room for any vehicles, and the shelves were full of an amazing amount of objects.

As Kate's eyes flitted over them, there was nothing she could recognise there. It all seemed to be pieces of metal and junk. Strange tubes with flanges on, bits of plastic ... nothing really identifiable.

Then she saw a large cylindrical container full of

some sort of greenish liquid. She looked closer and saw that suspended in the liquid was the largest maggot she had ever seen. At least she thought it was a maggot. On closer inspection it turned out to have a large single eye mounted on the front, above a pair of sharp-looking incisors. It was not a maggot!

'What is it?' Kate asked.

'No idea,' said Cavendish. 'It was there in the store.'

'Why did you take it?'

Cavendish tapped the jar. 'Because I could. UNIT didn't know everything about me. When I came out of hospital, I bought this place. I felt drawn to it. No-one knows I'm here, so no-one can come and debrief me.

'I wanted a slice of power . . . and then I started seeing ghosts. I'm not stupid. I can put two and two together . . . ghosts don't exist . . . but other things do.'

'I'm starting to see what you mean,' said Kate. 'But what? I saw him too. A man. He walked past me, and through a locked door . . .'

There was a sound from outside, a grinding, grating noise like concrete rubbing against concrete.

Kate and Cavendish both looked at each other.

'What was that?' asked Kate.

'No idea,' said Cavendish, his eyes flicking to the door.

'We'd better go look,' said Kate, and led the way out of the garage.

•   •   •   •   •

In the far future, the High Executioner was not at all happy with how things were progressing. There were power fluctuations, they could not maintain control of the totem, and there were also blocks and obstructions coming from something else in that timezone too.

She had called up more acolytes to focus the power and to allow the portal to be inched wider and wider.

She also realised that the focus of gaining more

power would be this man Cavendish, and how far they could push him. He was a man, and so finding his weakness should be easy.

She needed a female touch here though, and so had sent Eva for preparation. The girl had gone willingly, as these acolytes were bred to obey, brainwashed their entire lives to serve the Sodality.

Now she was returned. What remained of her was held in a copper cradle as with the man who had been controlling up to now. But her body was held within a human-shaped lattice of metal, copper and wires. Around the whole set-up was a dark red cloak, so that anyone looking quickly might just see the shape of a person, and not wonder at what abomination was hidden beneath.

One of the team quickly connected the copper wires, and added her to the focus around which the other acolytes were still circling, steadily chanting and making sure the power was as steady as could be managed.

The final connection was made, and the thing that had once been Eva opened her eyes wide and screamed. But it was a cry of satisfaction and hunger, not pain. Her nerve endings had been seared and she could no longer sense pain.

'She is near,' reported Eva. 'We can feel her.'

The High Executioner nodded. Things were coming to a head.

· · · · ·

Kate and Cavendish returned around the cottage. Nothing was out of place as far as they could see, but when they arrived at the front, Kate stopped dead.

Before them, sitting on the lawns, was the statue from the clearing.

'Now, that wasn't there before!' said Kate under her breath.

Cavendish held back as Kate stepped forward. 'Can

we go back inside now please? There's nothing here.'

'I want to know how this statue got here from the clearing.'

Kate looked around at Cavendish. She wasn't sure what all this was about, but what she was sure of was that it wasn't normal. She had seen a ghost. A real life ghost. And watched him walk through a solid door.

She had seen a garage full of alien machinery and alien creatures pickled in formaldehyde. That wasn't something she would quickly forget!

And now, here was another dilemma. This statue.

She moved closer to it.

'Last time I touched this thing, something happened. I was . . . somewhere else. It was terrifying. But maybe . . . maybe we can learn more about what's happening.'

She reached up her hand.

'I'm going to touch it again. If anything happens . . . anything at all . . . you will help me won't you?'

Cavendish gave a flash of a smile and nodded.

Kate reached out, felt the familiar static prickle as her hand approached the cold stone, and touched the statue . . .

•   •   •   •   •

Kate was immediately back in the red tinged, smoke filled place. There was faint movement around her, and the sound of chanting filled the air.

As she was expecting this, it didn't faze her as much as last time. She stood her ground and looked around, trying to make out something of where she was.

She heard a voice break through the noise. It was deep and calm.

'The portal is now open. Psionic science is superior. We can start the ritual.'

Kate looked around but there was nothing to see. She heard another voice break through. Cavendish.

'Kate? Kate?'

Kate could just make out something moving around her, and she reached out her hand to try and clear the smoke.

'Who's there? I can't see you?'

The strange asexual voice sounded again, and this time the message it carried was more worrying.

'We no longer need the man . . . now as the power builds, we will animate the totem . . . the movement was successful . . . next will be transformation . . .'

As she looked around, trying to find the source of the voice, a hooded shape moved into view before her. It seemed to be a monk of some sort. It stepped forward and stood before Kate, its head bowed.

As Kate watched, it slowly raised its head, and Kate saw what was hidden beneath.

The ravages of a once-pretty face. Metal and wires digging deep into the skin, and eyes held open by copper cradles. The mouth cruel and lips missing, revealing grinning teeth . . .

Kate screamed . . .

•   •   •   •   •

. . . and was lying on her back in front of the statue in the cottage garden.

Cavendish was kneeling over her, looking down in concern.

'Kate? Kate?'

Kate groaned. 'What happened?'

'You touched it, and then went rigid . . . Then I panicked and ran at you, knocking you away.'

Kate shook her head. It was hard to remember what had happened herself. She had just a blur of being somewhere else, and of seeing *something* . . . but then nothing.

She looked at Cavendish sitting on her. 'Would you mind?'

He smiled and got up, then helped her up. Kate

brushed herself down, and looked at the statue.

'I don't know what that thing is, but I'm not touching it again! Let's get back inside.'

They made their way back into the cottage, while the statue sat on the lawn. Immobile. Waiting.

8
Meet the Ghost

The night can be very long when you spend it either sitting on a chair, or lying on a sofa.

As dawn broke, Kate stretched and uncurled from the sofa where she had slept. Across the room, Cavendish stirred in his favourite armchair. He rubbed his eyes and looked around the room.

'Oh my back,' said Kate, groaning. 'I hate sleeping on a couch.'

She looked at Cavendish. 'At least nothing else happened... did it?'

'I don't think so.'

Cavendish cocked his head and listened. 'The voices in my head. They're not there.'

'When I touched the statue, someone was saying that they didn't need you anymore.'

'What did they look like?'

Kate thought a moment. 'I only got a glimpse... deformed... twisted... that was enough!'

'Not our ghost then,' said Cavendish.

'No... this was someone else.'

'Remember yesterday? We saw the ghost and he seemed to be trying to talk to us. He does that a lot.'

Cavendish curled back up on his chair. 'I think he's following me. Stalking me. I can't make it stop. I can't...'

Kate interrupted him: 'Douglas. We'll have a proper look around. For starters, what's through that door? A basement?'

Kate left the room and stood by the locked door.

'I don't know... that is, I've never been down there... it's locked.'

'I know it's locked. Where's the key?'

Cavendish looked at the ground. 'I . . . I threw it away.'

Kate looked at Cavendish, exasperated. 'Why did you do that?'

'I don't . . . I just want it to stop.'

Kate shot Cavendish a look. 'Then we've got to find out what's happening here. Look, before that ghost appeared, there was some sort of mist coming from under this door. There was a mist around the statue, and in that . . . that other place I went to.'

'Do you think they're connected?'

Kate cocked her head to one side with a *What do you think* expression on her face.

'We *really* need to see what's on the other side of the door.'

Kate thought a moment, then headed off down the hall towards the front door.

'I'm going outside to see if I can find some tools, or maybe another way under the cottage. It should be safe enough now it's daylight. Will you be OK?'

Cavendish just stood looking at her and after a moment nodded. 'Yes. I'll be fine.'

Kate paused with her hand on the front door, then, after a moment, returned to the living room and picked the leather-bound book up off the table.

'Just in case, eh?' she said with a smile.

Then taking the book she headed off outside.

Left alone, Cavendish took a deep breath and, looking at the spirits and glasses on his side table, wondered idly if it was too early for a shot. His eyes moved to a calendar on the table. It was October 31 . . . All Hallows' Eve.

He shuddered, and went to sit back down again. His eyes caught his own reflection in a mirror hanging on the wall, and he paused, looking into his own eyes.

He looked tired. Tired and unshaven.

He yawned and ran his hand over his bristles. Nothing that a good hot bath and a shave wouldn't cure.

He was about to sit down again, when there was movement elsewhere in the mirror, and Cavendish found himself looking at the ghostly man.

Cavendish whirled around, but the room was empty, There was no-one there.

He turned again and looked back in the mirror, but the ghost was still there . . .

A panicked expressed crossed Cavendish's face, but the ghost spoke, and this time Cavendish could hear him.

'No, don't run. Please don't run. Can you hear me?'

Cavendish swallowed. There appeared to be no immediate threat.

'Yes,' his voice cracked as he spoke. 'Yes. I can hear you. But . . .'

'There's no time,' said the ghost quickly. 'It's the mirror, reflects and conserves power. I'm trapped, trapped in time . . . you have to help me . . . us.'

'Help you? How?'

'I know you think you caused all this, but you're not to blame. Trust me.'

'Trust *you*?'

Cavendish looked at his own reflection again, and back to the ghost standing behind him.

'I'm really cracking up now,' he said to himself.

'There isn't much time,' said the ghost, 'you have to listen.'

'Okay,' said Cavendish. 'I'm listening.'

'I come from the future,' the ghost said. 'Your future. And Hell is on Earth. A powerful faction of revolutionaries called the Sodality seized power. They'll kill anyone who stands in their way. They're committed to control and corruption. They use the science of an ancient race of beings called Dæmons, and they're unstoppable.'

'But who are you?'

'In my era, we were called "Time Channellers". With the aid of our Time Sensitive companions, we roamed history. But the Sodality killed me, destroyed me with psionic power. Now I have only this wretched half-existence, living in the past times I have visited. But it's not all lost.

'This time—this day—is key. It's a crucial nexus point. With your help, we can frustrate the Sodality's plans and start to give the future a chance.'

Cavendish shook his head. This was a lot to take in. 'But you said this Sodality controlled the future?'

'There are key moments where conditions are right to summon the Dæmons themselves. They've opened portals back through time. That's where they'll gain the greatest power of all.

'There are other Time Channellers, people like me who can avert the death of the future before it becomes irreversible.'

Cavendish looked at the image of the ghost in wonder. 'Am I one? Am I a Time Channeller?'

The ghost looked sadly at Cavendish. 'No,' he said, shaking his head. 'No. You're a vessel, someone weak and broken enough to be controlled by the Sodality. They used you to help open the way, but it's not too late!'

'What can I . . . we . . . do?'

The ghost looked around. 'I need the book. It has power we can use.'

'Kate took it. She . . .'

At that moment there was a loud scream. Kate was in trouble. Cavendish turned from the mirror, and the ghost faded from sight.

9
Doubles

Kate left the house, and with a wary glance at the statue, which was still in the same place on the front lawn as it had been last night, headed round the back towards the garage of curiosities. Maybe there was something there which would help her get the door open. After all, a garage was where you kept tools, wasn't it?

She opened the door, flicked on the dim light and stood for a moment looking at the clutter.

She placed the book safely down on one of the shelves, and started to sort through the rubbish, hoping to see something she recognised.

There was a familiar creaking, grinding noise from outside, and Kate looked up. There was nothing to see. What she didn't see was the face of the gargoyle looking in through the cobwebbed window of the garage.

• • • • •

Having spent the last few hours compiling some of the most complex psyonic incantations that she had yet tried, the High Executioner had again assembled her acolytes after allowing them some rest. She knew from her augmented team that the humans in 2003 were resting, and so there was no hurry. But they needed to be ready when they awoke.

And now that time had come.

The chanting acolytes berated and summoned the power of the Dæmons, focussing it and channelling it. Whereas it was relatively simple to bring a stone creature to life in the same zone as you yourself were present, to do this over a 583 year difference, *and* to change the very form of the stone itself, was another undertaking.

As the power grew, so the High Executioner watched and waited. The time was approaching the key nexus point. And she had realised too over the last few hours, that the time was right for a summoning. Quite how that might work, she wasn't sure. The last time they had summoned a Dæmon, back in Venice in 1586, the creature had rejected them, promising to return a thousand years later, very soon as it happened in the High Executioner's current time zone. But 2003 was just 417 years later. How might it react?

The creature which had been Eva moaned with pleasure. She had sent her essence back through the portal to enable their totem to change appearance.

It had started.

•   •   •   •   •

Back in the garage, Kate was under attack. The whine of psyonic forces was getting louder and louder, and the shelves and the items upon them were starting to rattle and shake under the onslaught.

Kate crouched to the ground, her hands over her ears as the power grew and grew.

The vibration made the items start to fall from the shelves. Kate saw a futuristic chest unit fall, as well as a strange rubber doll-like creature. There was even one of the fabled shop-dummy arms clattering to the ground.

Suddenly, the heavy container in which the alien maggot was stored bounced off the shelf and fell, catching Kate a glancing blow on the head.

Kate screamed and fell to the floor, unconscious, as the power and noise rattled around her.

She didn't see the door to the garage slowly open, and a stone, hoofed foot step inside.

The hoof twisted and melted into the shape of a trainer-clad foot, and a monstrous leg made from mottled stone became more shapely and clad in denim.

The door to the garage closed behind whatever had entered, and suddenly, with a flash of brilliant white light, the noise and shuddering stopped.

The garage door opened again, and Kate stood there. At least it looked like Kate.

The creature looked back at the slumped form of the real Kate on the floor, smiled a cold, chilling smile of triumph, and headed off for the house.

10
Charm Offensive

Cavendish left the relative safety of the living room, and stood in the hall by the locked door. He could see that the strange icy white mist was creeping from under the door again.

There was a click from the front door, and he looked up to see Kate standing there.

She smiled at him, and sauntered into the hallway, one hand playing with her hair.

'Hi,' she said. 'I'm bored with this. Can you come and play awhile?'

Cavendish looked puzzled. 'I heard a scream. Are you all right? Did you find any tools?'

Kate looked directly at Cavendish. 'Scream did I?'

'Well *someone* screamed.'

Cavendish headed for the front door, and opened it again, checking outside. He saw that the front garden was again empty. The statue had gone.

Kate put her hand on Cavendish's arm. 'You know, Douggie, we just spent all night together here . . . and you never once really noticed me.'

Cavendish closed the door and looked at Kate.

'What do you mean?'

'Well?'

'Well . . . I . . .'

'Come on,' chided Kate. 'I know you like me.'

Cavendish nodded. 'I do . . . yes . . . but . . .'

'What?' teased Kate.

She was slowly moving towards Cavendish, but he in turn, unnerved by this new turn of events, was slowly backing down the passageway.

'I never get what I want . . . but I like you, Kate, I

really do . . . but . . .'

Kate reached out and stroked Cavendish's face gently.

'You're so cold . . . so cold . . .' he said as her fingertips touched him.

'Maybe I need warming up?'

Cavendish started to realise that something was very wrong here, and continued to back away.

'No . . . it's not . . . I'm not . . .'

'What, Douggie? Don't you want me?'

'Yes . . . no . . . I . . . I don't know . . . keep away.'

'Aww. Doesn't Douggie want to play? What a spoilsport.'

Cavendish wrapped his arms around himself, confused and upset by the way Kate was acting.

Then, her face cleared, the smile dropped from it. She stepped close to him again, and began one of the chants that Cavendish knew so well from the voices in his head.

'*Bmal elttila dahy ram . . .*'

This was the final straw. 'You're not Kate!' said Cavendish.

The creature stopped chanting and returned Kate's smile to its face. 'I could be . . .'

'No!' Cavendish stepped back again, falling to the floor in his confusion.

'No matter,' said the creature coldly. 'It's time. You've been struggling far too much . . .'

'No. You're not Kate! Not Kate!'

'Of course I'm not Kate!' said the creature. 'I'm here to give you what you want . . . and in return, I just need to take a little from you.'

The figure stretched out her arm towards Cavendish.

·   ·   ·   ·   ·

In the garage, the air seemed to shimmer, and the form

of the ghost stepped from thin air and approached the prone form of Kate.

'You have to wake up,' he said, holding his solidifying hand over her head. Kate stirred and groaned.

'Oh, my head!'

The ghost looked back towards the cottage. 'Come on, while there's still time!'

Kate pushed herself into a sitting position and shook her head.

'What hit me?'

She spotted the glass container and the alien maggot spilled out on the floor, surrounded by green goo.

'Aahh.'

'Don't be afraid, I won't hurt you,' said the ghost.

Kate blinked and pulled back. She looked the man up and down. 'I can see you,' she said. 'And hear you.'

'I'm an echo, that's all, a living echo of a possible future.'

Kate felt the bump on her head and winced. 'I've heard crazier things today.'

'Then listen. The power is building. The portal from the future is opening wider and wider. We can use that power.'

Kate stood up, her legs were a little shaky but she felt fine considering.

She tuned in to what the ghost was saying. 'We? That's as in "us"?'

The ghost nodded. 'But the Sodality are strong. They're intent on summoning the Dæmon.'

Kate shook her head. This was all too fast for her. 'Whoa . . . no, no, no. Hang on. Dæmon? Portal?'

'A passage between times.'

'Oh, right.'

'The Sodality used that to influence your friend to fetch the spell book. They used psionic power from the incantations to animate the statue. Here, in this time.'

Kate nodded. 'I think I got in the way of that.'

'We must hurry. The statue has shifted. It's hunting the final power to secure the Sodality's future.'

The ghost looked carefully at Kate. 'You're all right?'

Kate nodded.

'Let me see if there's anything here we can use . . . There must be something.'

Kate looked at the shelves once more. There was nothing obvious. She talked to the ghost while she checked the shelves.

'So if these Dæmons interfere with Earth's development . . .'

'They are scientists and explorers. They dabble when it suits them . . . they've no specific agenda to cause destruction.'

'You come from the future?' Kate eyed the ghost sceptically.

'Where the Sodality rule using the Dæmon's powers. Yes.'

'And they've followed you here.'

'Not really. They have limited control over time and space. They enslaved other Time Channellers. But I refused to cooperate. That's why they killed me. I still exist in the times I visited. And I can try and disrupt their plans. When I saw you arriving, I couldn't let you just walk away. I need your help.'

'I figured that.'

Kate hissed in exasperation. 'There's nothing here.' She picked up one object that had caught her eye. A small jar filled with . . . 'Unless we're expected to throw jelly babies at them?'

'You have the book,' said the Ghost.

'Well . . . I . . .' said Kate.

'I saw you take it,' he continued.

Kate moved to the shelf where she had placed the book. It looked so ordinary: assuming a centuries-old tome of alien magic could be called ordinary.

'I had to get it away from Douglas,' she said.

'Good,' said the ghost. 'Its power is not easily read.'

She picked up the book. 'Can we get rid of it?'

'Better that we use it. Good or bad. You can use it for either.'

'Me?' said Kate with a smile. 'I don't do spells!'

The ghost looked at her levelly. 'Who else is there?'

•   •   •   •   •

The creature looked at Cavendish on the floor of the hallway. He was half-sliding, half crawling to try and get away from it.

'What are you?' he said, 'Are you a Dæmon?'

The creature laughed. 'You want to see the form of the Dæmons?'

As it spoke so its image shifted around, becoming a monstrous shape composed of smoke and fire. Red eyes burned in the faded replica of Kate's face. After a moment, the form restabilised into that of Kate.

The creature smiled again. 'Scary, aren't they.'

She reached Cavendish and took his hand. He could feel a static tingle as she did so.

'*I* am controlled by the Sodality, rulers of Earth. Their power is older than time itself, from the shapers of Humanity. But you . . . with your inquisitive mind and acquisitive nature . . .'

As the creature spoke, so Cavendish felt as though his life was draining from him. An immense tiredness suffused him, and he felt that trying to resist further would be hopeless.

'That's right,' said the creature. 'Let the power flow through me.

'. . . *you* who were led to remove an ancient tract of summoning from where it had been secured . . . *you* have helped us release *their* power . . . and now . . . we want to reward you.

'Now we need the Horned Beasts to grow.

'We need life force to summon them. Their experiment was a triumph. *We* are the result. And this place shall be our temple to them...'

'You're insane,' gasped Cavendish.

'Not insane,' retorted the creature. 'We will have what we always deserved... *total* control... *total* power.'

The creature noticed that Cavendish was not looking at it any longer. Instead the human was looking beyond, to the door to the cottage.

The creature turned, and saw that the ghost and Kate were standing there.

'You cannot stop us,' said the creature.

'Now I think you can hear me,' said the ghost. 'We have the book...'

There was a ripple in the power field as the creature, and by reference, Eva and the High Executioner 583 years in the future, recognised the object.

'The book is ours by right.'

'But it's not in *your* hands.' The ghost nodded to Kate who held the book up in front of her. They both started to move slowly down the hallway towards the creature and Cavendish.

The creature turned to face them and raised a hand. 'By the power of the Sodality,' it said, and then began the chant of power: '*Regna nik cab koolt nod...*'

Kate felt the book start to get hot. She held it more tightly as yellow and gold light started to fleck the edges.

A faint stream of energy could be seen flowing through the air from the creature to the book. They were draining it!

The creature staggered, but found some purchase. '*Regna nik cab koolt nod...*' it chanted again.

At that moment, Cavendish, released from the drain of his own energy, launched himself at the creature and distracted it.

Kate and the ghost, the book glowing brightly and emitting ice white mist from inside, hurried past the creature and the ghost opened the formerly locked door.

It swung open revealing bright light and white mist which billowed around them.

Past the door was a set of wooden steps leading down. Kate took one look back and hurried down, closely followed by the ghost.

Back in the hallway, the creature rocked as it reorientated itself.

Then, with a contemptuous glance at Cavendish who was still cowering on the floor, it too opened the door and descended the steps.

This fight was not over.

PART THREE

1
The Caverns

Heading down the steps, Kate could feel the air chill considerably. No wonder the mist which came from here was icy! There was a frosty breeze from somewhere deep underground, and Kate's flesh broke out in goosebumps.

She reached the bottom of the flight of steps and paused.

There was a tunnel leading further on, with rough, rock-hewn walls and ceiling. As though the very bedrock on which the cottage stood had been carved out.

Behind her, the figure of the other Kate appeared, and Kate moved on quickly down the tunnel, clutching the still-warm book to her chest almost as a ward to the icy chill.

The tunnel suddenly split and opened out, larger cave-like tunnels headed off in different directions, and Kate paused, not quite knowing which way to go.

The ghost suddenly stepped from one side, and indicated a direction. With a hesitant glance behind her, Kate followed.

After a few minutes, and more changes of direction as the tunnels split, Kate emerged into a much larger area. This was more like a cavern than a tunnel, and the ceiling was far overhead.

To one side was a low, flat rock, and on it, the remains of what once had been an altar of some sort. There was a ragged cloth bunched up on one side, and some scattered black candles. Kate even saw what looked like a knife resting there.

Everything was covered with dust and cobwebs. It was obvious no-one had been down here for some time.

'What is this place?' asked Kate.

'It's long been a magnet for those who would try and gain power,' said the ghost, inspecting the paraphernalia.

'What should we do?' asked Kate.

'Set the altar. Use the book. Try and stop the Sodality.'

'Is that all?' said Kate. 'Not much then.'

'Quickly,' said the ghost. 'I can't touch anything, you will have to do it.'

Kate set the book down and started to assemble the altar, straightening the cloth and setting the candles upright. She picked up the knife carefully.

'As long as we don't have to actually kill anyone.'

'That shouldn't be necessary,' said the ghost. 'Quickly ... they're nearly ready.'

'I'm going as fast as I can,' said Kate, placing the knife back on the altar and positioning the book between the candles.

•   •   •   •   •

In the future, in the shell of St Paul's Cathedral in London, the High Executioner of the Sodality grinned.

In front of her, the two converted acolytes were focussing all the psyonic power on the portal, and the summoning rituals.

Now their totem: the statue; was in the caverns themselves, the power was clearer, and the energy that they had absorbed from Cavendish had been enough to kick-start the ritual.

The High Executioner remembered back to Venice, when they had been surprised that the Dæmon they summoned, Mastho, claimed to have been summoned before. This made no sense at the time—clearly no-one from the Sodality had summoned him, or they would have known about it.

The only prior summoning on record was the one in Devil's End around 1973, but that was the Dæmon Azal, and the man behind it, calling himself Magister, was not one of the Sodality, but a stranger to them. However it was he who consolidated the rituals and summonings and who created the book that they now used. Quite how he did this or how he knew so much, the High Executioner had no idea. Nor did she much care.

All that mattered was that from the Dæmons' point of view, this was to be the first arrival of Mastho on Earth...

The creature that had once been Eva, and who was now connected to the totem in 2003 via the steadily increasing portal, moaned with pleasure, as the power grew, and her ability to operate increased with it.

•   •   •   •   •

The creature wearing Kate's body finally arrived at the same cavern where Kate and the ghost were setting up the altar.

It laughed at them.

'Ignore it, Kate,' said the ghost.

'The time is right,' said the creature. 'We shall summon the Dæmon *now*...'

The creature straightened and closed its eyes, its mouth moving silently as the incantations to summon the Dæmon were intoned.

Kate looked at the ghost urgently. 'What now?'

'We need to find the counter. Flip through the book!'

Kate started to turn the pages of the book on the altar as the ghost watched and scanned each. After a moment he stopped her.

'That one!'

Kate looked at the page. 'But that's just a blur, the characters are all shifting about!'

'Give it a moment,' he said.

'I can see it!' said Kate. 'I can read it I think!'

She narrowed her eyes and started to speak the strange language that she saw. It was as though she thought the words and then found that she could speak them.

'*Llams dnat aerg serut aercl la . . . llal ufitu aeb dnath girbs gnih tlla.*'

On the other side of the cavern, the creature started to frown and tremble.

•   •   •   •   •

Eva frowned and started to struggle in her network of copper and cables. There was something battling her control of the creature in 2003.

Her mind started to flood with images of normal life, of something she had never experienced: green grass; live animals; clean air; sunshine.

'Fight it,' said the High Executioner through gritted teeth. 'Fight it!'

Eva drew on more power from the circling acolytes, and fed it back through the portal to their creature.

•   •   •   •   •

'It's working,' said Kate as the creature started to stumble.

'Don't lose it,' warned the ghost. 'Keep going!'

Kate dropped her eyes to the page but the symbols were all over the place again.

'*Lla . . . lla . . .* I can't read it! I can't see the words!'

'Come *on* Kate. You can do it. The book will channel the power.'

The creature smiled as Kate faltered, and then elegantly dropped to one knee in the cavern.

Her form shimmered, becoming, briefly, the dust and fire image of the Dæmon before shifting back to the form of the gargoyle statue.

As Kate watched, there was a wet, ripping, tearing sound, and the smoky form detached itself from the statue and rose, rippling, in the cavern.

'We're too late!' said the ghost. 'The portal is

widening ... the Beast is coming through!'

'Not if I can help it,' said Kate, picking up the book, and once again holding it in front of her. She approached the solid form of the statue.

As she approached, so the words from the book formed themselves on her tongue.

'*Llams dnat aerg serutaerc* ... *lla lufitu aeb dnath girbs gniht lla.*'

A line of power suddenly emitted from the statue, hitting the book square on. There was an orange flare of power, and Kate lost her footing, tripped and fell onto the statue ...

   .   .   .   .   .

... and appeared sprawled on the floor of St Paul's Cathedral.

She scrambled to her feet and looked around.

As before she was in a place lit with red. It was full of dust and noise. Chanting and movement of people.

The scale of the building was lost in darkness, but around her Kate could see figures moving in a circle.

To one side stood the slight figure of a girl, or perhaps a woman. She was wearing boots and some sort of tight outfit, and her head was partially covered with a velvet cowl. Kate could see her mouth though, which was curved in a cruel smile. It was obvious that she was somehow in charge here.

A voice said: 'The Dæmon has been summoned. Increase the power. Maintain the connection!'

Kate turned to see who was speaking, and saw again the 'person' she had seen before. The shattered and broken remnants of a man held together with technology that she could not pretend to understand.

Beside him was another figure, again broken and torn and stitched back together again.

The girl/woman at the side brought her hands together as though she was praying. 'The Dæmon ... it comes...'

Kate whirled again as the Acolytes increased their chanting.

'*Eco eco daha elttil bmal ... eco eco daha elttil bmal.... eco eco daha elttil bmal!*'

Kate looked around, trying to see and make sense of anything here, but it was hopeless. There was too much confusion and pain.

'*Eco eco Mastho! Eco eco Mastho!*'

The woman's cold voice echoed through the chamber. 'As my will so mote it be!'

Kate began to panic as the shattered man said: 'She knows much, but not enough.'

Kate struggled to her feet. 'What is this place?' she asked, more to herself.

She moved over to where the acolytes were circling, and pulled at one of them. The person seemed to be in a trance or something and did not react.

Kate looked around again. Her gaze fell on the booted woman who was watching the proceedings intently, a cruel expression on her face.

She frowned when she saw that Kate had seen her.

A voice behind Kate said: 'She sees us!'

Kate turned again to see that the shattered man had spoken.

She moved closer to the man and the woman who were sitting in the nightmare of copper and wires, all of it intertwined with the skin and flesh of their bodies.

'What do you want?' Kate asked.

'Question irrelevant,' came the answer from the woman.

'Locus point moving!' said the man.

'What is happening?' said the woman standing outside the circle as the chanting faltered and broke.

'The Dæmon is coming,' said the shattered woman calmly. 'But not to the intended date. The locus point is changing now to the date of this creature's departure.'

Kate shook her head. 'Creature? I'm not a creature.

I'm a human. Like . . . like you.'

The chanting suddenly picked up again. It grew louder.

'Locus point established. Now 2003. The Master is coming.'

Kate looked around again. There seemed to be nothing she could do.

The sound rose, an internal screeching which made her head hurt.

Kate brought her hands to cover her ears against the cacophony, and then suddenly . . .

2
The Dæmon

. . . she was back in the cavern. Cavendish was beside her and he had dragged her from touching the statue, which was still there, crouched and immobile beside them.

The book was lying on the floor nearby, so Kate, shaking her head to try and clear it, picked it up.

She looked at Cavendish who was pale and weak, but managing to hold himself together.

'You okay?' she asked.

Cavendish pulled himself up and gave a curt nod. 'Fine. Can't let these things get on top of one.'

He smiled briefly at Kate.

They both turned and looked at the centre of the cavern, in which a whirling, roaring column of matter was coalescing.

There was a roaring groaning sound, and a deep rumbling as though the Earth was groaning. There was a final shudder and the cavern fell silent.

Before them stood the form of what Kate could only assume was a Dæmon.

It stood about eight feet tall, a terrifying demonic presence shrouded in darkness. Its goat-like eyes glowed red, and it had curved horns set in a ring around its face. It had no mouth, just a pulsing dark set of vertical slits through which a yellow, sulphurous smoke or steam was being emitted. Smoke billowed all around it, making it seem far larger than it actually was.

The creature cast its head around, looking at those in the cavern. There was a gentle hissing sound as it moved.

Then. It spoke.

'Who has summoned me here?'

Its voice was loud and forceful, that of a creature not

used to being challenged, or perhaps summoned.

The air flickered, and Kate saw that the figure of the ghost, who had been standing, solid, before the altar, started to fizz and fade, as though he were a television picture which was rapidly being de-tuned.

'No . . . no . . . there is . . . energy drain . . . I . . .'

His voice faded in and out before he faded from view entirely, before returning again as a faint outline.

The Dæmon watched all this, moving its head and arms as though it were an insect hunting for food. Still one moment, then fast and strong the next.

Eventually, Kate found the creature's gaze resting on her. She held the book protectively to her.

'I sense the powers which have brought me here. They are from a distant time.'

Kate continued to stare at the creature in astonishment.

'You . . . you have the smell of power on you. Why have you summoned me? Am I to be questioned?'

The Dæmon took a step towards her.

'Who . . . what are you?' she asked finally.

'I am Mastho,' answered the creature. 'From a world many light years distant. My people watch as you puny humans play at life.'

Behind Kate, Cavendish seemed to come to his senses. He had been watching the Dæmon, and sensed that this was, in part, one of the powers which had sought to control him. But not *the* power. This was infinitely more dangerous. But he had played some part in this alien *thing* being brought to Earth, and he felt that he could also help stop whatever it was that it was here to do.

He took the book from Kate, and, holding it in his arm, started to flick through.

'Must stop this,' he muttered to himself. 'Must stop. All my fault.'

The Dæmon looked at Cavendish with interest, and Kate, seeing the interaction, decided to try and distract the creature. It was all she could think of doing.

'Who are your people? Have you been here before?' she asked, stepping away to the other side of the cavern from Cavendish. The Dæmon's head turned to regard her, and it stepped towards her once more.

'We have been summoned many times. We are interested in how our experiment progresses. We like to see how this planet responds to our input.

Kate was now getting very confused. *Experiment*?

'But why are you here now?' she asked.

'It amuses us to indulge the whims and caprices of you humans. In other times we are worshipped as gods . . . I was summoned here by those who would perhaps seek to control me.'

Kate reached the far side of the room, and she looked across to where Cavendish, and the faded form of the ghost were standing.

Cavendish looked up in triumph. 'No. I have it . . .'

He smoothed out the page of the book, and started to read. 'We must stop this . . . this evil!' he said.

The Dæmon, Mastho, swung its head back to regard Cavendish.

'Evil? What evil? We do what we do for the sake of science . . . if there is some judgement over our interest, then that comes from the heart of man.'

Cavendish glanced at the creature, then looked at the text. '*Emac uoy ecn nehw mor fecalp eht ot nomead nruter nruter . . .*'

There was a grating sound, and Kate realised that the creature was laughing.

'You, the one called Cavendish . . .'

Cavendish looked up briefly but continued his chant.

'You have more energy for me,' said the Dæmon. 'You are broken, and a broken vessel bleeds faster than a sound one . . . Ahhh . . . What do you seek? What is your broken heart's desire?'

Tears ran from Cavendish's eyes, and the Dæmon gestured with one of its hands to the stone statue of the gargoyle which was still crouching, immobile, where it had ended up. There was a hiss and glow of light, and the statue morphed into the shape of Kate herself!

The statue walked across the cavern, smiled at the Dæmon, and approached Cavendish.

He had stopped speaking, his mouth and lips dry. His eyes were locked on hers as she approached, raised a hand, and gently stroked his face, brushing away one of the tears.

'What is it you want? You want this form? You want companionship? An end to loneliness? To despair? To feeling unwanted, and unloved? Give me those feelings, that power.'

As she spoke, so Cavendish seemed to deflate, his face turned ashen grey, and his knees trembled, taking him down to the cavern floor.

'That's right,' said the gargoyle. 'You're a good, good man.'

With Cavendish down, the gargoyle moved over to the Dæmon, and knelt by its feet, looking up at it.

Mastho drew in a deep breath, smoke and flame-lights flickering around it. 'Power . . . freedom . . .' it sighed.

Kate narrowed her eyes. This wasn't right. Cavendish had done nothing wrong.

'. . . from a good man,' she said quietly.

The Dæmon paused, and then, with a hiss of smoke and roiling fumes, it moved towards her. She stood her ground, trying hard not to scream, as the creature came close to her. It regarded her for a moment, and then raised a hand and, with the gentlest of touches, brushed her own cheek.

There was a crackle of energy and Kate stepped back as though she had been punched in the stomach. A rush of golden energy trailed from the Dæmon's fingers and back to Kate as it tasted her essence.

The Dæmon dropped its hand.

'Your father would know what to do . . .' it said

simply. Goading her and reading her and understanding totally where her loyalties and beliefs lay.

Kate straightened up. She felt drained, but she was not going to let this . . . Dæmon or whatever it was start to talk about her father in that way. She knew that it was trying to destabilise her. To break her in the same way it had broken Cavendish. That wasn't going to happen.

'My father is a good man,' she said. 'As is he.' She gestured to Cavendish. 'And if you feel you've won, after having fed on his desires and hopes, then so be it. But I don't have to stay and watch.'

Kate gave a look back at the Dæmon, then turned her back on it and walked unsteadily towards the cavern entrance. Sometimes retreat was the better part of valour.

3
Discussions with the Devil

As she left the main cavern area, Kate again felt the chill breeze on her skin. She walked along the roughly hewn tunnel, wondering how she would find her way out again.

There was a strange rushing sound, and, as she turned a bend and came to another open area, the Dæmon was standing ahead of her once more.

'Explain yourself,' came the powerful voice.

'Why?' she said. 'Can't you tell when there's more important things at stake than power? Don't you have a heart? Look at what you have taken . . . perhaps you'll find the answer there. But I doubt it.'

Kate took a deep breath. If you were going to argue with a Devil-God then you'd better make it a good argument, she thought.

She stopped and looked up at Mastho. 'If you're going to destroy the Earth, or whatever it is you *want* to do, then I *want* to be with the people I love. My son. My dad . . . That's more important than arguing with you.'

The Dæmon regarded her for a moment, and then a chuckling sound echoed around the caverns. Kate realised that the creature was laughing.

'That is an interesting observation, human. Power causes you to react in different ways.'

There was a movement behind Kate, and she turned to see the gargoyle creature appear behind her, but still looking like herself. It was very disconcerting.

The Dæmon looked at the gargoyle. 'Ahh . . . my channel to the future. What have you to say? I will allow you back into the control of those who sent you . . .'

The image of Kate flickered gently, and she rocked

on her feet before stabilising, her face taking on the hard look which she had seen before in the cottage.

'Power,' said the gargoyle, 'is whatever humanity makes of it. You are simply the catalyst, not the cause or the reaction.'

·   ·   ·   ·   ·

In St Paul's Cathedral, the shattered woman spoke the same words as the gargoyle uttered in 2003.

'. . . not the cause or the reaction.'

The High Executioner muttered some psyonic incantation under her breath, trying to gain full control over her creature.

'We are so close,' she said. 'Mastho, the Dæmon, is with them, and we must gain full control. We must be seen as the worthy successors of its power.'

She looked at the acolytes, slowly circling them. 'Increase the ritual of binding!'

They started a slow rhythmic chant, cabbalistic words designed and planned to capture the Dæmon and bind it to their will. Or at least to root it to one place and time so they could work further on proving that they should be the ones to receive its great power.

·   ·   ·   ·   ·

Mastho regarded the gargoyle Kate with interest.

'. . . the Portal is still open. I can feel the Sodality probing, testing me with their rituals and their bindings . . .' It sounded thoughtful, impressed that these humans from the future could even do such a thing.

Kate looked at the Dæmon. What argument could she use which might make it turn away. What was it that it wanted anyway? She realised that she actually had no idea what this massive Devil-like creature wanted. Why was it on Earth?

She plucked up courage and asked the obvious

question: 'So what do *you* want?'

The creature seemed to waver and flicker as it searched for the answer. '*Cavendish* was lonely . . . despairing . . . he wanted . . . he wanted . . .'

Kate was interested that it seemed to be looking for the answer in Captain Cavendish's memories. Maybe that was it. The creature had been summoned using his power, so maybe it was being driven by some of Cavendish's desires as well.

'Love?' she blurted.

At this, the gargoyle laughed and stepped forward to confront the Dæmon alongside Kate.

'I . . . I cannot recognise that,' said Mastho. 'But there is much which interests me.'

'We are taking what is rightfully ours,' said the gargoyle. 'The power to control this zone, to extend our worship of you through all times. Love does not come into it.'

Kate could recognise the voice of that long-haired woman who seemed to be in charge in the future in what the gargoyle said.

She considered all that she had seen. In particular the business with the Great Intelligence at the University. Some good people had become infected with its power, but whatever it wanted to achieve had been thwarted.

'But power corrupts,' said Kate. And then, remembering her own love for her father. 'Love heals. A world without love is pointless.'

The gargoyle looked at her. 'Love is transient. Humans die every day, love unrequited. Pathetic.'

Kate was not having this. 'But love transcends death,' she said. 'Why do people mourn? Because they have lost something precious and valuable. Because they *continue* to love.'

Mastho the Dæmon nodded his great head, seeming to take in and understand what Kate was saying. The gargoyle saw this too, and chipped in:

'Don't listen to her. She's trying to trick you. You

have been summoned by the Sodality . . . you must obey.'

The Dæmon turned its attention to the gargoyle. 'Obey? You . . . what are you? An artifact controlled from the future by those who would seek my power. Do *you* know this thing called love?'

'With power there is no need for love.'

The rumbling laugh again echoed through the caverns and tunnels. 'Power . . . power! Is that all your puny minds can conceive?'

The gargoyle looked concerned, and frowned as it received further instructions from the future.

It crouched on the ground and started to intone a further psyonic incantation.

'Eco eco dah a elttil bmal . . . eco eco dah a elttil bmal . . . eco eco dah a elttil bmal.'

Kate looked from the gargoyle back to the Dæmon. What would it do now?

'So go on then,' she called bravely. 'Do whatever it is you were summoned for.'

The creature looked at Kate. It found these humans fascinating. No wonder their great race had chosen this planet for its experiment. Even though the humans thought they understood, they actually knew little of the Dæmon's great plan . . .

'The Sodality want my power to control this temporal zone,' it said thoughtfully. 'Even now they are preparing to take it. But I am a Dæmon, and they *dare* to try and shackle me.'

It looked again towards the tunnel which led to the main cavern where Cavendish had been left.

'Love . . . You humans are fascinating.'

It turned back to Kate. 'Three times I can be summoned. This Sodality forgets this. Perhaps they need reminding . . . and their portal works both ways . . . The experiment continues.'

With that, the huge creature raised a hand and touched the gargoyle on its head. The gargoyle stopped chanting and screamed, both it and the Dæmon fading away as the scream echoed through the caverns.

Then all was silent.

Kate looked around. There was no sign of the Dæmon or of the gargoyle thing. It was cold, and the breeze blew against her. She breathed out and saw her breath steaming in the air.

She turned and made her way back down the tunnel to where she had left Cavendish, all the time wondering what his departure meant.

4
Endgame

The High Executioner was not happy with how things were progressing. She could not understand how the Dæmon could be so interested in love. It was not a concept that played any part in the Sodality. It was all about power, and the need to capture the power from the Dæmons so that they could rule the Earth unopposed.

In St Paul's Cathedral, there was a shudder in the rocks underfoot as the energy that they were sending to maintain the portal and the gargoyle in 2003 was suddenly returned to them.

The air around them darkened and a wind blew up inside the building, drawing dust and rubble towards a centre point where the energy was being focussed.

The High Executioner recognised this from the Dæmon's last appearance in Venice, 1586. The Dæmon was coming.

Some of the acolytes were dragged in also, screaming as their bodies were crushed to a pulp, their blood and bone forming part of the swirling maelstrom.

The two control elements: the shattered man and woman, sat in their cyborg cradles, all emotion had been purged in their conversion to the cause, so now they just sat and observed.

There was a massive rumble, and the huge form of Mastho appeared in the church, towering over them all. Its goat-like hooves clattering on the stone floor, and sending chips of paving and debris in all directions.

'Where is the one in control!' roared the Dæmon. 'I would speak with them.'

There was a moment's silence as the remaining

acolytes all scurried for cover.

The High Executioner stepped forward. 'I am in charge.'

The Dæmon considered her for a moment, and then spoke.

'In my timeline this is the first time I have been summoned. You know already that you may summon me but three times.'

The High Executioner looked at the Dæmon and smiled. She had already summoned this creature once before in her own, somewhat convoluted, timeline, back in 1586, and was familiar with the process and appearance. It didn't stop it being quite terrifying though.

'I know this, Lord Mastho,' she said.

The Dæmon paused and looked around. 'So this is what your power has wrought so far,' it said. 'Death. Destruction. Fear.'

It shook its head. 'You humans ...'

It turned and moved closer to the High Executioner.

'Know this, little human,' it said. 'This will be your death and your salvation. You may not be able to see what is to come, but for us it is as simple as flicking through the pages in a book.'

The High Executioner frowned, not quite grasping what the Dæmon was saying.

'But ... I ...'

'Silence!' cried the Dæmon. Its voice echoed in the church and as it faded, there was indeed silence.

'You play with me further, and I will deem this experiment a failure, just as I suspect my brother Azal did before me. Now leave me!'

The Dæmon watched as the acolytes hurried for the exit. The High Executioner gestured to two of her handpeople, and they pushed the trolleys on which the shattered man and woman rested out as well.

As she turned to leave, the High Executioner bowed deeply. 'My Lord,' she said, before turning and sweeping out of the church.

Left alone inside the chamber, the Dæmon Mastho gathered his energies, and prepared for the return trip to his homeworld.

Humans were so amusing. But not one of them had yet guessed the true purpose of the experiment. But they would. Very soon. At his third coming on Earth, all would be revealed.

Mastho didn't think the humans would like it. But that wasn't his problem. And indeed, he didn't even consider it further, just as a human pouring boiling water on an ant colony never considered what an inconvenience this might be for the ants.

The spectral winds and power grew as Mastho prepared to step back through the dimensions to his own world. The air grew cold as the energy was sucked from it, and ice formed over the floor by his feet. With a roar of power and an inward rush of air to fill the void left by his body, the creature vanished.

Epilogue

Kate entered the main cavern chamber to find Cavendish sitting up, his back against the crude altar.

Beside him was the ghost, standing as always and looking concerned and very faint.

Cavendish looked up at Kate as she entered. 'You managed to distract him then.'

Kate frowned. 'I'm not so sure,' she said.

'And we're safe,' said Cavendish, more as a reassurance to himself.

'For the moment,' agreed Kate.

Cavendish seemed to slump. 'Thank you Kate,' he whispered.

'That . . . creature, Mastho. It seemed very sure of itself. And three times it said . . . does that mean it will be back?'

There was a fizzing noise like a radio being tuned, and Kate heard the ghost speaking to her.

'It will be back . . . just not in your lifetime,' he said.

'What about you?' asked Kate. 'Will you be alright?'

'Who can say,' said the ghost. 'Power . . . three . . . my own . . .'

And then he faded from sight.

'Does that mean we won?' wondered Kate.

She helped Cavendish to his feet and together they staggered to the entrance of the cavern. Kate looked back. Everything was quiet. The massive leather-bound book was lying open on the altar.

Kate left Cavendish propped against the wall, and returned to the book. She looked at it but the symbols were once more unreadable.

She closed the cover firmly.

'I think we will keep that closed,' she said.

Then she returned to Cavendish and the two of them

limped back through the tunnels, heading for the steps leading to the cottage.

For the moment, the adventure was over.

BEHIND THE SCENES OF 'DÆMOS RISING'

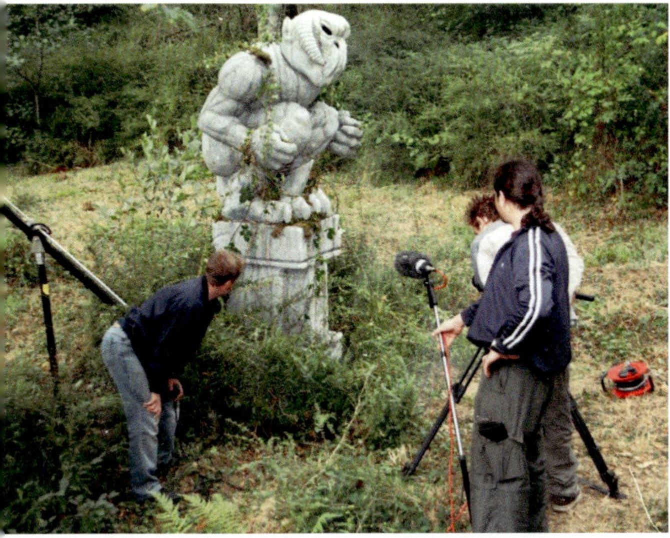

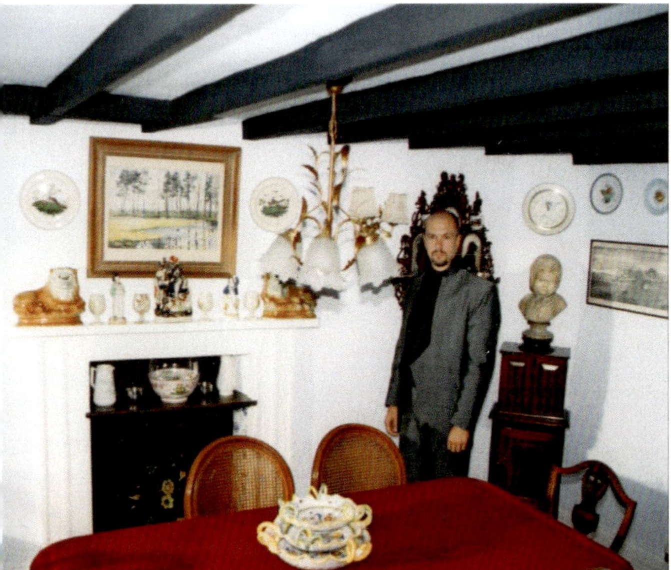

CAPTIONS TO PICTURES

1. The main cast: Miles Richardson (Douglas Cavendish), Andrew Wisher (The Ghost) and Beverley Cressman (Kate Lethbridge-Stewart). With 'friend' looming behind!
2. Producer and Director Keith Barnfather with Beverley Cressman on the roads leading to the cottage.
3. Beverley with the directions to the cottage.
4. Miles Richardson tries to summon up supernatural help.
5. The Gargoyle statue made by Philip T Robinson.
6. Keith, Lighting Cameraman Neil Osman, and Sound Recordist Luis G Garibey with the Gargoyle statue in the grounds of the cottage.
7. Andrew in position for a 'faded' shot of the Ghost in the cottage.
8. Miles recording a scene in the hallway of the house.
9. Keith and Editor Anastasia Stylianou go over the storyboards for the next scenes. (Pic: Robin Prichard)
10. Beverley and Andrew with the Grimoire of Psyonic power. The book was made by Bob Covington.
11. Kate and Cavendish check out something nasty in the garage.
12. Cavendish is seduced by the Gargoyle posing as Kate.
13. Beverley in the caverns which were dressed with cobwebs and planks.
14. Keith directs Andrew and his time-travelling companion (Amanda Evans) in the caverns. They are about to be killed!
15. Beverley with the hooded Sodality Monks outside the entrance to the cavern.
16. Andrew and Beverley in the caverns.
17. Andrew and Beverley share a joke in the caverns between takes.
18. Cast and Crew relax at the end of recording. L to R: Rosemary Howe (Production Assistant), Neil Osman (Lighting Cameraman), Anastasia Stylianou (Editor), Keith Barnfather (Producer/Director), David J Howe (Writer), Andrew Wisher (The Ghost), Beverley Cressman (Kate Lethbridge-Stewart), Miles Richardson (Douglas Cavendish), Luis G Garibey (Sound).

All photos taken by David J Howe unless otherwise stated.

About The Author

David J Howe has been involved with *Doctor Who* research and writing for over thirty years. He wrote the book *Reflections: The Fantasy Art of Stephen Bradbury* for Dragon's World Publishers and has contributed short fiction to *Peeping Tom*, *Dark Asylum*, *Decalog*, *Dark Horizons*, *Kimota*, *Perfect Timing*, *Perfect Timing II*, *Missing Pieces*, *Shrouded by Darkness* and *Murky Depths*, and factual articles to *James Herbert: By Horror Haunted* and *The Radio Times Guide to Science Fiction*. Another notable work of fiction is *talespinning,* a collection containing David's many short story pieces and screenplays.
www.howeswho.co.uk

STAY ON

Here are details of other exciting TELOS titles. If you cannot obtain these books from your local bookshop, or newsagent, then please check the website below.

TELOS PUBLISHING,
www.telos.co.uk.

FILM TIE-INS

THE DÆMONS OF DEVIL'S END
Sam Stone, David J Howe, Raven Dane, Jan Edwards, Suzanne Barbieri and Debbie Bennett; with special picture 'Dossier' by Andrew-Mark Thompson
978 1 84583 969 7   A Telos Adventure

OLIVE HAWTHORNE is the sole guardian of the sleepy village of Devil's End. She protects the world from the incursion of demons, vampires, aliens and all manner of otherworldly creatures. But she is getting old . . . and they keep coming . . . This is the story of Olive's life. From her earliest days, through teenage years, middle age, and now old age. Tales of her adventures with monsters and evil . . . forever battling against the forces of darkness . . . and forever seeking to keep the world safe.

SIL AND THE DEVIL SEEDS OF ARODOR
Philip Martin
978 1 84583 979 6   **A Telos Adventure**

SIL is worried, very worried, which doesn't keep his reptilian skin in the best condition! Confined in a cold detention cell on the Moon, awaiting a deportation hearing for trial over drugs offences on Earth, he faces a death sentence if the application is successful and he is found guilty. And his employers at the Universal Monetary Fund aren't pleased either. Not at all.

As time runs out and friends desert him, Sil must use all of his devious, vile, underhanded, ruthless and amoral business acumen to survive.

Can he possibly slime his way out of this one?

FICTION ORIGINALS

HELEN MCCABE

THE PIPER TRILOGY
1: Piper
2: The Piercing
3: The Codex

SIMON CLARK
Humpty's Bones
The Fall

DAVID J HOWE
Talespinning
Horror collection of stories, short novels and more

RAVEN DANE

THE MISADVENTURES OF CYRUS DARIAN
Steampunk Adventure Series
1: Cyrus Darian And The Technomicron
2: Cyrus Darian And The Ghastly Horde
3: Cyrus Darian And The Wicked Wraith

Death's Dark Wings
Stand alone alternative history novel

Absinthe & Arsenic
Horror and fantasy short story collection

SAM STONE

KAT LIGHTFOOT MYSTERIES
Steampunk adventure series
1: Zombies at Tiffany's
2: Kat on a Hot Tin Airship
3: What's Dead PussyKat
4: Kat of Green Tentacles
5: Kat and the Pendulum
6: Ten Little Demons
The Complete Lightfoot (limited hardback edition of all six novellas, plus bonus material)

THE JINX CHRONICLES
Dark science fiction and fantasy, dystopian future
1: Jinx Town
2: Jinx Magic
3: Jinx Bound

THE VAMPIRE GENE SERIES
Vampire, historical and time travel series
1: Killing Kiss
2: Futile Flame

3: Demon Dance
4: Hateful Heart
5: Silent Sand
6: Jaded Jewel

Zombies In New York And Other Bloody Jottings
Horror story collection

The Darkness Within: Final Cut
Science fiction horror novel

Cthulhu and Other Monsters
Lovecraftian style stories and more

GRAHAM MASTERTON
The Djinn
The Wells Of Hell
Rules of Duel (With William S Burroughs)
The Hell Candidate

DAWN G HARRIS
Diviner
Supernatural horror thriller

FREDA WARRINGTON
Nights of Blood Wine
Vampire horror short story collection

TANITH LEE
Blood 20
20 vampire stories through the ages

Death Of The Day
Standalone crime novel

Tanith Lee A-Z
An A-Z collection of short fiction

STEPHEN LAWS
Spectre

SOLOMON STRANGE
The Haunting of Gospall

RHYS HUGHES
Captains Stupendous
Steampunk adventure novel

PAUL LEWIS
Small Ghosts
Horror novella

PAUL FINCH
Cape Wrath & The Hellion
Terror Tales of Cornwall ed. Paul Finch
Terror Tales of Northwest England ed. Paul Finch

If you have enjoyed this book and would like more information about other TELOS titles, then check the website below.

TELOS PUBLISHING
www.telos.co.uk

WATCH THE ORIGINAL DRAMA

AVAILABLE FROM AMAZON, ALL DVD RETAILERS, AND FROM

www.timetraveltv.com